T.A. Maxwell

The Zen Lunatics

The Zen Lunatics

Printed in the United States of America
First Printing, 2013
ISBN 0-9890182-0-3

Published by Zen Dog Publishing, U.S.A.

ta.maxwell@live.com
www.amazon.com/author/tamaxwell

For Jack Kerouac

The Zen Lunatics

"I want to see the Space Needle," I announce out of the blue as I lie sprawled out on the living room couch in my blue plaid boxer shorts, shirtless. Empty beer cans, wine bottles, an ashtray full of cigarette butts, and a six inch clear plastic bong litter the top of the used coffee table I picked up at a local Goodwill last summer.

"Okay," says my friend and roommate Drew, who is lying on the love seat in his favorite pair of Superman tighty-whitey underwear, also shirtless. He is a recent convert to the Zen lunacy that is our way of life. And by our, I mean myself and our other roommate and friend Barry, who is only called that by his family, we call him Bear. He is sitting in the comfy, puffy green chair in his tie-dyed robe, which he stole from a not-so-classy hotel in Santa Barbara a few months back and which he tie-dyed himself. He, of course, is wearing nothing underneath and is half asleep. We are all hung over, watching an episode of House Hunters International on HGTV.

"Well?" I say.

"Well what?" asks Drew.

"I want to see the Space Needle."

"Well get on the computer, find a picture of it, and look at it."

"No man, I want to see it in person."

"It's in Seattle dipshit," adds Bear, who I thought was asleep, but apparently he was just resting his eyes or possibly in deep meditation.

"No shit, I know where the Space Needle is."

"We are in Los Angeles. Seattle is like a thousand miles away."

"It's actually more like twelve hundred miles Drewski. We could be there by this time tomorrow, come on guys."

"You're fucking crazy Max, why the hell would we spend all that money on gas and food and lodging to look at a structure we can see on the internet?"

"Because a picture is shit man, it's nothing. Seeing it in person is spiritual, it's like real live crazy meditation, you can't get that from a picture. We can even go to the top of it and look out and see Puget Sound and Mount Rainier, and fucking Canada man."

"You're crazy man, but what the hell, let's do it, Bear you down?"

"You know I'm down. I love Zen lunatic road trips. Especially to the great northwest," Bear's eyes are still closed and he is quite possibly still in some sort of meditative state.

"Fuckin' A, lets pack," I yell.

We each pack a bag, which include the essentials; clothes, a toothbrush, and deodorant. I pack the toothpaste. Drew packs the protection, for possible violent and/or sexual interactions. And Bear packs the weed. It is late April and the weather is great in L.A, but I suggest we each bring a light jacket just in case. The weather in the great northwest can still be a little chilly this time of year. After a couple of hits on a small joint and a quick snack, which is just a bowl of Lucky Charms, we head to the car, our packs in hand. It is almost noon on a Monday. We jump on Interstate 405 and head north, Bear is in the backseat, Drew is in the front passenger seat, and I am behind the wheel of my black 1996 Jeep Cherokee.

"I might get fired for this Max," Drew says with a slightly concerned look on his face.

"Nah, just call in sick, tell them you got that flu bug that's been going around."

"I don't know man, I told them two weeks ago I had the worst case of Hershey squirts in recorded history and I don't think they bought that shit. The next day at work my boss just looked at me and shook his head like he knew I was bullshittin'."

Drew works at a small popular grocery chain in West Los Angeles. Bear used to work there too, that's where they met. I knew Drew from high school and met Bear through him. Drew's boss is a dick, a total douchebag. He spends his entire shift hitting on the female workers and yelling at the male workers, trying to impress those chicks with his authority and shit. He thinks he is so fucking cool, but he's not, he's a fucking manager at a grocery store, there is nothing cool about that.

"Fuck him man, he can suck my dick," Bear chimes in from the backseat. The guy fired him for opening boxes of food and eating it on the job, so he is not a fan of his.

"Yeah fuck him, I'll write you a legit doctor's note and it will be all good man," I add.

"Yeah fuck that motherfucker," Drew yells as he cranks up the stereo, which is playing Lynyrd Skynyrd's *Sweet Home Alabama*. We all sing along, even Bear, whose eyes are still closed, possibly still meditating, as we head north on Interstate 5 through the Grapevine.

I don't have to worry about being fired, because I don't have a job. Well that's not true, I'm a writer, but don't tell my father that's a job, at least not a real job. "Anyone can write boy", he would say to me every time he asked me what I was doing for work and I told him I was writing. I would always reply with "yes they can father, but that doesn't mean they can write well."

My relationship with my father is somewhat complicated.

He left when I was eight and disappeared for fourteen years. Then one day, out of the blue, he called me. I was a week away from graduating from college and he wanted to come and watch me walk across the stage since he missed it when I graduated from high school. Why? I still don't know, but I told him he could do whatever he wanted, I just didn't want to talk to him before or after. He agreed and when the day came all I could do was search for him in the crowd.

I don't even remember the speeches or even walking across the stage, all I remember was looking, searching for my father in the stands, not even knowing who I was looking for. I never saw him, at least I don't think I did. A couple of weeks later he called again and I agreed to meet him for breakfast.

The meeting was mostly just us eating with a little conversation in between the chewing, all of it initiated by him. He apologized for leaving and not keeping in touch, but said that he started a new family and was busy with that. All I said was that it was okay and that I had gotten over it the night of my graduation after hours of thought, along with some beer and weed. I left out the latter. He was glad and said he wanted to see me again. I said that would be cool and six years later we still keep in touch, mostly through phone calls and text messages. I have flown to Sioux Falls, South Dakota to see him and my step-mother and my half-brother and half-sister a few times. They are a nice bunch and I am glad that we could all reconnect and put the past behind us.

"What are you thinking about Max? Or are you in that

wide-eyed Zen meditative state you like to be in?" asks Drew.

"Just thinkin' Drew boy."

"And what are you thinking about Maximilian?"

"Oh just thinkin' about how drunk we're all gonna be tonight."

"Hells yeah Maximum overdrive."

"Did someone say drunk?" Bear interjects, his eyes finally open, wide, wider, widest, with his head coming towards me, smiling, and finally kissing me on the cheek. We all bust out laughing as we merge onto northbound Highway 99 and head into Bakersfield.

We stop at a local gas station in Bakersfield for some gas and snacks. Drew grabs the usual; some beef jerky and a couple energy drinks. Bear always gets a green tea and a bag of Funyuns. He thinks he is such a Zen lunatic because he drinks green tea. I always give him shit because Snapple green tea isn't fucking Zen, its corporate bullshit, the complete opposite of Zen. I grab a coffee, fair trade from some South American country of course, and an apple fritter.

After we gas up and grab our goodies, we continue north on Highway 99 instead of Interstate 5 because, well, Interstate 5 up through central California is a goddamn bore-fest, just cow farms and rolling hills. At least on Highway 99 you drive through several towns on your way up to Sacramento, which passes the time a lot quicker. Just north of Bakersfield I see a hitchhiker.

"Let's pick him up."

"Who?" asks Drew as he looks around.

"That hitchhiker." I point at a guy walking north on the right side of the highway as we pass him.

"No way man. You know you're not supposed to pick up hitchers man."
I pull over on the gravel shoulder about a hundred yards ahead of the hitchhiker.

"Dude, this is not a car full of chicks. We are three men, he's not going to fuck with us," I explain as I extend my left arm out the window and wave him to come on. I look back and he is jogging towards the Jeep, almost there.

"Besides, we could use the road karma."

"Road karma?" asks Drew.

"So we don't blow a tire man or die in an accident," Bear chimes in.

The hitcher jogs up to the front passenger window.

"Hop on in man," I say, shooting my thumb towards the backseat as Bear, without direction, scoots over and sits behind me.

"Thanks man," the hitcher says as he opens the rear passenger door and climbs in.

The guy I am guessing is around our age, mid to late twenties, but he looks older because of all the dirt on his face and clothes. It's not like he's covered in dirt, but you can tell that he has been on the road for a while. He is wearing a pair of tan chino pants and a blue and green plaid cowboy type shirt. He is also wearing a navy blue bandana that is keeping his dirty blond dreadlocks from attacking everyone in the vehicle. He has a moustache, one of those handlebar jobs but it's scraggly and could use some wax. His pack is an old army pack that he probably got at an army surplus store somewhere.

"Thanks again man, I really appreciate it."

"No problem. Where you headed?" I say.

"San Fran."

"Alright, well we are headed to Sacramento so let's see how close we can get you." I grab the road atlas I have had for years and start thumbing through it.

"So what's your name fellow traveler?" Bear questions.

"Well my given name is Joe, but my friends all call me Crazy J."

I turn my head away from the map and look at Drew whose eyes are as wide as the Grand Canyon staring right at me and non-verbally telling me, I told you so.

"Why do they call you that?" I inquire.

"Well, the crazy part is because I'm always doing crazy shit like those Jackass guys. You know jumping off of shit, skateboarding naked, shit like that. And the letter J is cause my name is Joe, so..."

Drew's eyes relax and I go back to examining the map.

"So what's your guy's names?"

"Drew. Introductions please," I say still trying to figure out the best place to drop Crazy J off.

"Okay. Well I'm Drew." He points at himself. "That's Bear." He points at Bear. "And this is Max." He points at me and I give our new temporary companion the thumbs up.

"Nice to meet you guys."

"Alright Crazy J, it looks like Manteca is the best we can do. From there you just have to hitch a ride straight west and you should be in Frisco in no time."

"How far to Manteca?" Drew asks.

"Looks like about a three hour drive, two and a half if I get a little heavy on the pedal."

"Sounds perfect man, you guys are lifesavers."

"So, you smoke, Crazy J?" Bear asks as he opens his eyes.

"Smoke what?"

Bear's eyes open wide and then wider as he slowly leans in towards Crazy J and says in a Vincent Price voice "Weeeeeeeeeed."

"Yeah man, why?" Crazy J says slightly terrified. Drew and I try hard not to bust out laughing.

"Cause if you didn't, we were gonna have to kill you and turn your skull into a bong." Bear could not keep it up and started laughing before he could even get the word bong out of his mouth. Drew and I follow and all three of us laugh uncontrollably for a good three minutes. Crazy J didn't know what to think of the scene. I thought for sure he would jump out and take off back towards Bakersfield running hysterically, but he didn't. He went from slightly terrified to super terrified to laughing with us.

"Bet you didn't think you were going to catch a ride with a bunch of Zen lunatics when you woke up this morning did you?" I say while smiling at him through the rearview mirror.

"Sure didn't."

"I think you need a little wacky weed my brotha," Bear says to Crazy J.

"I think we all need a little of that my brotha," I add.

"I second that," chimes in Drew.

"I third that," proclaims Bear.

"Well, roll that shit up and let's get our asses on the road," I say as I put the Jeep into drive and merge back onto northbound Highway 99 kicking up gravel and a cloud of dust in the process.

We make a quick pit stop in Visalia to use the bathroom. By now we have a good little buzz going from the joint we shared, so Crazy J runs in to grab some munchies as the rest of us load back into my Jeep.

"We should take off and leave him," says Bear.

"What the hell for?" I say.

Bear, now in the front passenger seat leans towards me and whispers "because he's a fucking hippie and I hate fucking hippies."

I lean in towards him, our noses almost touching and whisper back "dude, you are one more tie-dyed shirt away from being his brother, brother." I smile and give him a little head butt.

"Fuck you man, he stinks, fucking patchouli and B.O., its killin' me."

"We should fuck with him," Drew interjects.

I turn my head towards the backseat and say "what's on your mind Drew screw?"

"How about when he gets in the car I will say that we are out of smokes and I need to run in and grab a carton. I will pay for them but I will run out of store like I stole them and then we take off."

"I like it, let's do it," I reply.

Just as I say this Crazy J exits the store, walks to the Jeep, opens the rear passenger door, and climbs in. Right when he shuts the door the plan goes into effect.

"Shit man, we're out of smokes. I'm gonna run in real quick and grab a carton for the road."

"Yeah, you better, we're gonna need some smokes," I say.

Drew exits the car from the left side, jogs around the front of the Jeep and enters the store. Not thirty seconds later he bursts out of the store holding a carton of smokes, sprinting towards us. He violently opens the right rear passenger door.

"Scoot over man, quick, quick, quick," Drew yells, breathing heavily. Crazy J quickly scoots over with a confused look on his face. Drew slams the door.

"Go, go, go," Drew yells.

I had already started the Jeep when he went into the store, so I put it in drive and peeled out, ass hot, out of the parking lot and got back onto Highway 99 heading north.

"What the fuck Drew? Tell me you didn't do a grab and run?" I yell.

"Hells yeah I did Maxi man," Drew smiles and then looks

at Crazy J, serious face style and says "You don't have any warrants, do you?"

Crazy J, still in shock, takes a few seconds to respond. "Warrants? No man no warrants, but shit man I don't want to go to jail."

Bear looks out the back window, "Shit man is that a highway patrol cruiser back there?"

Drew and Crazy J turn quickly and look out the back window. I look at the rearview mirror and by God if there wasn't a highway patrol car three cars back in the other lane. This prank could not have gone any better up to this point. Hell, even I had forgotten that this was a joke and thought to myself shit we are fucked, which I repeated out loud.

"Shit, we are fucked."

Bear added "fuck man, I still have a shit ton of weeeeeed on meeeee." At that I started to think that I should probably drive the speed limit, because even though the cigarette theft was a joke, Bear did have a shit ton of weed on him and I was still a little high. We did not need to be stopped by no hi-po.

By this time, Crazy J was shitting his pants, probably literally, the guy did stink.

"Hey, you guys need to look forward, if you're all looking at him he is gonna know something is up," I say. They all turn back and face front. I look at the rearview mirror and notice that Drew looks a little nervous, too nervous.

"Drew, you alright?"

"You gotta get off this highway man, like now," he says.

He is starting to sweat and freak me out.

"And why do I need to do that? You did pay for the smokes right?" Crazy J looks at Drew and then back at me trying to figure out what is going on.

"Yeah, I just didn't pay for this Zippo lighter." Drew holds up a shiny silver Zippo lighter. Crazy J is beginning to realize what is going on.

Bear jumps in "You dumb bastard, you know we have weed in here, fuck."

I take the next exit, just north of downtown Selma, and the highway patrol car exits right behind us.

"Cop's exiting too, he is fucking right behind us, shit." I say. Crazy J turns and looks out the back window.

I yell "Dude, what the fuck are you doing, face front, face front." I take a right fully expecting to see blue and red lights behind me. No lights. I pull into a Burger King parking lot. No lights. The highway patrol car continues down the road. We are safe, for now. I pull into a space and turn the Jeep off. I turn towards Drew.

"Dude, what is wrong with you? All you had to do was buy a carton of smokes, run out of the store, and jump in, simple, easy, and you had to make it an actual theft." Drew's frowny face transforms into a dipshit smiley face and he starts laughing uncontrollably. The three of us all look at each other like, what the fuck is so funny?

Drew laughing says "The Zippo is mine. I didn't steal it, I've had it for years."

"You motherfucker," yells Bear. I look at Bear and shake my head "this fucking guy," pointing my thumb at Drew. Bear and I start to laugh and as we laugh it continues to get louder. Crazy J is fucking lost.

"So did you steal the lighter?" he asks.

"No," replies Drew, still laughing.

"What about the carton of smokes?"

"Nope." We are all laughing harder now.

Crazy J is pissed and he grabs his pack from the back "you guys are fucking crazy man, I'm outta here, thanks for the ride." He exits the Jeep, slams the door, and heads into the Burger King.

"Bear, I think Drew is now officially, a Zen Lunatic."

"Yep, this crazy motherfucker got us good, a fuckin' prank within a prank, classic."

"Should we go in and apologize to Crazy J?" I ask.

"Nah, fuck him, he doesn't even deserve to be called crazy, he should change his name to Stinky J," Drew says and we all laugh.

"Shit, we should start calling you Crazy D," Bear added.

"Alright, fuck him, we gotta get to Chico by night fall anyway, let's get back on the road."

I start the Jeep, put it in reverse, and back out of the parking space.

"Chico? We stoppin' for the night?" asked Drew.

"What. I didn't tell you guys?

"Noooooo," Bear answers.

"I thought we were driving straight through to Seattle?" Drew added.

"Well, I thought we would all enjoy a little pit stop in Chico for the night so I called a college buddy of mine and asked if we could crash out and maybe hit up the bars tonight. He said it was cool, so it's on like Donkey Kong."

"It's Monday night man, are the bars even open in Chico?" Drew asks.

"I take it, Drewski that you have never been to Chico?"

"Nope"

"Well, I went to college there and I assure you the bars are open. The fucking college has always been rated a top party school and shit, all students do there is party. Hell, there was even a riot back in the 80's that shut down the town's Pioneer Days celebration forever. The bars are open bro."

"Well shit, lets rock n' roll," Drew yells.

Bear adds, "Step on it Max, I wanna see some titties."

I enter the on-ramp and we continue north on Highway 99 all the way to Chico. The four hour drive to Chico went by real quick. We jammed out to various songs on various radio stations, snacked on junk food, and threw back several energy drinks that made us fly high. We sang every song that came on the radio, if we did not know the words we made up our own or tried to guess what the singer was going to say. We did not do much talking, but we laughed every once in a while as we thought about Crazy J and the double prank that made him bolt, poor bastard.

CHAPTER TWO

It is eight o'clock and completely dark out, which is
making it more difficult to find Rob's house. We finally spot it,
but I pass it, so I turn around and park on the street right in
front of his place. We exit the Jeep, grab our packs, and hurry
up the walkway so we can get the introductions over and start
partying. I knock on the door and after waiting what seemed
like a full minute Rob answers it.

"Mad Max, what is up?"

"My dick. What is up with you Rob slob on my knob?"

We enter the house and Rob closes the door behind us.

"Damn, you haven't changed a bit, still a dick"

"I am what you eat."

Rob shakes his head and smiles and then points toward the couch, "Throw your bags over there, I'll grab us some beers."

Rob heads to the kitchen while we toss our packs next to the couch. We take a seat on the couch and wait for Rob to return with some ice cold refreshments. He comes back into the living room carrying four beers. He gives one to me, then one to Drew, then one to Bear, and opens his own and takes a drink. The three of us do the same.

"So, who is who here?" Rob asks as he takes a seat next to me on the loveseat.

"Rob, Bear, Bear, Rob. Rob, Drew, Drew, Rob."

"Nice to meet you guys," Rob says. Both Drew and Bear reply the same.

After the usual, what have you been up to, conversation that old friends endure when they haven't seen each other in a few years, we need a refill. I offer to get the next round and Rob tells me the beers are in the fridge on the bottom shelf. Just as I return with the cold ones, pass them out, and take my seat, the front door opens and in walks a super cute chick wearing cowboy boots, a mini-skirt, and a blue plaid cowgirl shirt with the sleeves rolled up. She is holding a shopping bag and looks stunned as she closes the door, probably not expecting to see a room full of guys.

"Hi," she says to all of us.

"Hi," the three of us reply in unison.

"Hey Caroline, this is my good buddy Max." Rob points at me and I raise my hand to say hey. "His friend Drew." He points at Drew, who does the same. "And his other buddy Bear?" He points at Bear and Bear nods to confirm that is his name.

Caroline replies, "It's nice to meet you guys, let me set this in my room and I will come back out and hangout."

"Cool," says Rob.

I look at Bear and Drew and open my eyes wide. Then I point to my chest and lip the word "mine" as to claim dibs on her. Drew shakes his head and I nod my head and give him my serious face. Drew gives me his mad face and lips the word fine. Bear doesn't care and I already know this because he likes trendy hipster Buddhist chicks who drink tea and ride bikes, not sexy cowgirls. I like sexy cowgirls and Drew knows this, which is why he gave in so easily. He also knows that there are going to be a bunch of chicks at the bars tonight and he doesn't want to spend the entire night trying to mack on this one chick, but I do.

I suddenly realize that Rob might already have dibs on her so I turn to him, lean in, and whisper "who the hell was that?

"That's my roommate."

"Are you two...?" I inquire, insinuating something between them.

Rob chuckles, "no man, we are just friends, go for it."

"She single?"

Caroline walks in the room, out of nowhere, holding a beer. "Yeah, I'm single" she says.

I turn beet red realizing that she heard what I had just

asked Rob. I look at her, smile, and shake my head. She smiles back, opens her beer, and takes a long drink. The girl of my dreams is right in front of me. This is going to be a great night or a fucking disaster. Rob offers his seat to Caroline and she takes it as Rob sits on the floor, smiles at me, and lips the words "you're welcome." I fucking love this guy I say to myself. We finish our beers and I volunteer Drew to get the next round, which he does.

"So where are you guys from?" Caroline asks.

"L.A," I answer.

"Ah, the city of angels, nice, so what are you guys doing in Chico?"

"We're headed to Seattle and thought we would stop for the night and hangout with Rob and party a bit."

"So how do you know Rob?"

"We went to college together."

"You went to Chico State?"

"Yep, I met Rob in a creative writing class junior year. We sat next to each other and one day we had to read and edit each other's work and we got to talking and the rest is history."

"Creative writing? What, were you an English major or something?"

"I was. I graduated with my bachelor's degree in English six years ago."

"Shut the fuck up. I'm about to graduate next month with my English degree."

"Shut the fuck up."

"No, really, I start the teaching program in the fall. I'm want to be a high school English teacher."

"Wow, you're brave. I could never teach high school kids, they're fuckin' savages."

"So what are you doing with your degree?" she asks.

"I'm a writer," at this, Drew chuckles.

I turn towards him, "what the fuck are you laughing at over there bucko?"

Drew replies, "What the hell have you written?" Knowing full well what I have written.

"You know. I wrote a screenplay." I hold up my right thumb. "I have written like fifty poems." I extend my index finger. "And I have started two short stories." I extend my middle finger and retract the others giving Drew the bird, "all of which you have read, dick."

"I have never seen any of that shit," Drew says, lying. He starts to chuckle.

I interrupt Bear who is talking to Rob, "Bear, tell her about my writing and poetry."

Bear looks at me, confused "What writing and poetry?"

"Man, shut the fuck up," I say, getting irritated.

"Oh yeah, I remember now, terrible shit, worst shit I have ever read." Bear says smiling.

"Dick," I say.

Bear laughing, "I'm just pullin' your chain, it's all good stuff man, good stuff."

I turn back towards Caroline "See what I have to deal with." I look back at Drew and Bear, "these two Zen Lunatic motherfuckers."

"What's a Zen lunatic?" Caroline asks.

I turn back towards her, "Um that is a discussion for later, after the bars, when we get back here and get high." I look at the guys and smile.

"Hells yeah," says Drew.

"Fuckin' A," adds Bear.

"Let's get this show on the road. Regulators," yells Drew.

In unison Rob, Bear and I yell back "Mount up."

Caroline laughs and shakes her head, "this should be an interesting night."

I look at her and smile, "it's gonna be epic."

We all hang out at the house a bit longer waiting for it to get a little later because nobody goes out before ten anywhere. I continue to talk to Caroline and ask her the usual, where was she from? (San Diego), where does she work? (at a local sandwich shop), etc. I also catch up with Rob and discover that he decided to come back to Chico last year after getting a job offer at a local law firm. I tell Bear and Drew not to get too excited, he is just a divorce and estate lawyer, nothing fancy. But don't let him fool you, he came back to date college chicks, no doubt. Rob did not disagree and asked us if we knew why he liked college girls, we said no but I knew what was coming, and he informed us that the older he gets they stay the same age. Fucking Rob and his movie quotes. *Dazed and Confused* was his favorite to quote, especially Wooderson.

While I caught up with Rob, Drew talked with Caroline. The majority of the conversation was Drew asking her about any friends she could call that would want to roll to the bars with us. She made a few calls and a couple of her friends agreed to meet us out in a couple hours. Bear was just sitting on the couch, drinking beer, eyes closed, I assume in deep meditation.

Right at ten we begin to get ready, which meant that us guys stood up and drank another beer while Caroline changed her outfit, put some make-up on, and did her hair. When she was in the bathroom, we started to get impatient so I yelled "I like ponytails, FYI." She exited the bathroom two minutes later with her hair in a ponytail. I smile and we head out the front door. As we walk to the first bar, their house is pretty close to downtown and all the bars, I couldn't stop smiling and neither could Caroline.

The first bar we hit up is Normal Street, which is always the first bar we go to, but we usually only stay for one drink. The one drink is our party starter, the infamous Adios Motherfucker, a concoction of multiple liquors and mixes. Actually, I have no idea what is in it but it tastes good and fucks you up. The next bar on the schedule is a Chico institution, Madison Bear Garden, which we simply call the Bear, which Bear gets a kick out of. It is Monday night and that of course means Bear-e-oke. We order the usual, a round of beers and the tastiest shot ever, the Wake Smacker.

We find a large stand up table with no stools to set our drinks down and claim as our home base in the front bar area. This bar has several bars and rooms, two downstairs, one upstairs where the dance floor and pool tables are, and one outside where the Bear-e-oke is going down. The crowd is not too big or too small, but a nice size for a Monday night. About twenty minutes in, two of Caroline's friends walk through the front door. Caroline sees them, smiles, and waves them over. Drew perks up and starts to process which one he wants to hit on. He nudges Bear with his elbow.

"Dude, which one do you want?" Like it's that easy, just pick one and it's on. But to give Drew credit he usually closes the deal.

"What?" replies Bear.

"Which one of Caroline's friends do you want? They are right there man." Drew points but not too obvious. "I like the brunette. You want the redhead?"

"Sure man, you know me, I'll bang anything."

Now Bear seems more Zen than lunatic, but the lunatic side, when it comes out, is a site to be seen, and bet your ass we will all see that side of him tonight.

"Gentlemen, these are my friends Tina and Courtney. Ladies this is Max, Drew, and Bear." Caroline points at each of us as she does the introductions. "And of course you know Rob."

We all say our hellos and then the girls all head to the bar for drinks.

Drew starts the questioning "So there are three of us and two of them, what's the plan? Rob do you have a history with either of those two or like either of them?"

"I banged Tina once," Rob says.

"Which one is Tina again?" Drew asks.

"The redhead."

"Oh, okay. Soooo do you want to take a crack at the brunette?" Drew inquires.

Rob thinks about it for a couple seconds, "Nah man, you guys have at it."

"Cool." Drew says and then he turns towards Bear "alright Bear boy I'm gonna take a crack at the brunette..."

"Courtney," I interrupt.

Drew looks at me, irritated, "Yeah. Courtney. Whatever." He looks back at Bear. "So, me the brunette, you the redhead, cool?"

"Sure."

The ladies return double fisting beautiful teal colored drinks, Wake Smacker cocktails I presume, which you can get as a shot or a drink. They set six of them on table and Caroline goes back to the bar to get hers. We grab ours and take a drink, sure enough it's a Wake Smacker and it is delicious. By this time we are all feeling pretty good and I am drunk enough to suggest going outside to the patio for some Bear-e-oke, which I would never do sober. Everyone agrees, so we head outside and take the only open table. Three girls are destroying Cyndi Lauper's *Girls Just Want to Have Fun* and we almost go back inside, but they finish and we decide to stay.

"So what song are you going to sing Mad Max?" Rob asks as I flip through the song book.

'I don't know man, I'm thinking of something that will melt faces and warm hearts."

All the guys laugh and the girls look at each other probably thinking, what have they gotten themselves into.

"Alright, I got one." I say and I head over to the DJ table and hand the women my selection. She says she will call my name when it is my turn. I give her the thumbs up and head back to our table. Caroline and I make eye contact and we both smile, she is so damn cute and I am sure my cheeks are flush red. Drew is talking to Courtney, more than likely give her his usual pick-up lines that are cheesy but for some reason work. Rob is talking to Tina and Bear is listening in, but doesn't seem interested in the conversation. Ten minutes pass and finally my name is called. I finish my drink, that is half full, and head over to the mic. The music begins and Caroline, smiling, shakes her head. The rest of our party recognizes the song and they all begin to shake their heads as well. I smile and begin singing.

"Where it began, I can't begin to knowin', but then I know it's growin' strong." Caroline is smiling and Bear begins to nod his head.

"Was in the spring, and spring became the summer, who'd have believed you'd come along." Bear walks toward me nodding his head faster now, the rest of our party is now

nodding their heads as is most of the people out on the patio.

"Hands, touchin' hands, reachin' out, touching me, touching you." The entire patio sings along with me.

"Sweet Caroline, bomp ba da, good times never seemed so good. I've been inclined, bomp ba da, to believe they never would, but now I..." Bear is dancing up a storm now, even though this is not really a song for dancing. The place is loud and everyone is having a great time. I finish the song, take a bow, and head back over to the table where a fresh beer is waiting for me. Bear is still dancing, with no music playing. Caroline shakes her head again and smiles at me.

"I'm sure I'm not the first guy to do that, but I had to."

"Actually I have had guys make mixed CDs for me with that song on it but that was actually the first time anyone has sang it to me."

"Well I wasn't gonna do it, seemed cheesy, but I thought what the hell it's a great fucking song."

"Well, I'm glad you did, it was sweet."

It was around midnight when we left the Bear and headed to our final bar of the night, LaSalle's. This has always been Rob and I's routine, Normal Street first, then the Bear, then LaSalle's. LaSalle's is the place where we like to dance off all the calories we have been drinking so far. As we approach the bar we can hear the music booming. Right when we walk in some chick is spinning the drink wheel and it stops on five dollar Adios Motherfucker pitchers, oh shit, here we go.

"Adios." I yell.

"Mothafuckaaaaaaa," yells Rob.

The girls all go "woo" and we head to the bar to grab our pitchers, one each of course, which should end our drinking for the night. Five minutes later we are all standing on the edge of the dance floor each holding a pitcher of blue deliciousness in one hand and a glass of blue deliciousness in the other. We are ready to tear this dance floor up. As we are standing there drinking and watching others dance I notice some drunk guy on the dance floor with toilet paper stuck to his shoe and I bust out laughing.

"What are you laughing at?" yells Caroline, having to yell because the music is loud as hell.

I point to the guy and say, still laughing "that guys has toilet paper stuck to his shoe." She notices it and starts laughing too. We nudge the others to include them in our fun and we all laugh, apparently loud enough for the guy to notice because he looks at us, but he doesn't know why and he keeps on dancing. Bear is the first to get on the dance floor. He posts up in the middle of the floor and starts doing the robot and we all start busting up. Rob joins him after he finishes off what is left in his glass. Then Drew joins them. I look at the ladies and say "well, here goes nothin'."

I set down my pitcher, finish what's left in my glass and shimmy on out to the center of the dance floor. All four of us are doing the robot to some hip-hop song and we are not anywhere close to being in rhythm and we don't care. We all face the ladies and robot wave them over. They are smiling as they throw back the rest of their cocktails and dance towards us as the song changes. We dance for an hour, Caroline and I continue to connect with each other. We shut the bar down and head back to Caroline and Rob's house.

On the way back to the house we decide to stop at a local twenty-four hour diner to grab some food. Our dancing has given us quite an appetite. The waitress seats us in a large booth that barely holds the seven of us. We order coffee and waters and look at the menus while she grabs our drinks. When she returns we all order an assortment of breakfast classics, including pancakes, waffles, eggs, bacon, sausages, hash browns, etc. When the food arrives we dig in, sharing everything. Drew is so hammered that he mistakenly puts ketchup on his pancake. He shrugs and eats it anyway. Bear puts a sausage in each of his nostrils and asks us if he has something on his face. The four of us guys all laugh as the ladies shake their heads and say "gross." Neither one of these guys is getting laid tonight. We are laughing so loud the waitress comes over and tells us we need to keep it down, she is getting complaints. We agree to lower the volume. Rob looks around to see who might have ratted on us, giving evil eyes to all of five tables in the place that are occupied by people.

"I think it was that older couple over there," he says loud enough for them to hear him as he points at their table, which is only about fifteen feet away. The man shakes his head and then looks down.

"Who cares man, we're done anyways, let's get out of here, we have some weeeeed to smoke." The latter I say loud enough for all in the diner to hear." The guys laugh, the ladies hide their faces. We pay for our feast and leave, arriving at the house within five minutes.

Everyone files into the house through the front door. The guys take seats on the couch, I head to the bathroom, and the ladies head to Caroline's room, probably to talk about us and what is going to go down in the next couple of hours. I finish up in the bathroom and head back to the living room where Bear has already began to roll the second of probably three joints. The ladies exit Caroline's bedroom and join us in the living room. Tina takes a seat in between Rob and Drew on the couch, interesting. Courtney takes a seat next to Bear on the loveseat and watches the master joint roller at work. Caroline stands next to me. Bear finishes the second joint and begins the third.

"How many you gonna roll up there buddy?" Rob asks.

"This is the last one, I figure one for you guys." Bear nods his head towards Rob, Tina, and Drew. "One for them." he nods his head towards Caroline and I. "and one for us." he nods at Courtney and himself.

"Sounds good to me," Rob says.

"Is that stuff any good?" asks Tina.

Bear looks at her like, what do you think? And says "this is the super duper mega blow your fucking mind shit. If Jesus was alive he would only smoke this shit."

We all laugh hysterically at this as Bear licks the sticky part of the paper and finishes off the third and final joint and hands it to Rob. He then picks one up from the table and holds it out towards me. I walk over, take it, and walk back over to Caroline. He picks up the first one he rolled and his lighter and lights it. He takes a huge hit, holds it in for a few seconds, and exhales a huge plume of white smoke.

"You guys have a lighter?" Bear asks as he passes the joint to Courtney.

"Yep," Rob answers.

"Of course," I say, pulling my lighter out of my pocket and showing it to him.

Rob lights his joint, takes a hit and passes it to Tina.

I turn to Caroline. "So, you wanna smoke this on the roof?" She has a confused look on her face.

"The roof?"

"Yeah, I noticed how clear the sky was tonight on our walk home, thought it would be cool to chill on the roof, smoke this joint, and enjoy the stars."

Rob interjects "enjoy the stars? You fag." Bear and Drew laugh.

I smile and chuckle because I realize how lame that sounded but I stick to my guns. "What are you two laughing at?" I say to Bear and Drew. "I have spent all day being a lunatic, it is time to get my Zen on. Rob you got a fucking ladder?"

"Yeah, it's out back in the garage."

"Cool." I place the joint behind my left ear and say to Caroline "let's go." She nods her head and we head to the garage to grab the ladder.

The garage is fairly clean and I see the ladder almost immediately. I grab it and swing it around almost hitting Caroline in the head, but she is agile and moves out of the way just in time. We walk to the side of the house and I prop the latter up against the house.

"Ladies first."

She grabs the ladder and begins to climb. I hold the ladder steady so she doesn't fall and also so I can get a good look at her ass as she ascends. She looks back and catches me, I smile, and she smiles back, as she continues her climb. She gets on the roof and I follow. We find the flattest spot on the roof and lay down. I take out my lighter and then remove the joint from behind my ear. I light it, take a hit, and pass it to Caroline who does the same. We look up at the sky, it is a clear night and it seems that every star is saying hello to us.

I start the conversation, "someone told me once that stars are not actually stars but holes in the sky and the light we see is actually Heaven. And when we die our soul floats up and enters Heaven through the nearest hole. I know that's not true, but I like the idea. Can you see all the souls floating up towards the holes?"

"Yeah, and I like that idea too. I hope when I die that's what happens. It sounds nice. You know what's crazy?"

"What?" I take another hit of the joint and pass it back to

Caroline.

"The stars we see right now might already be burned out. They are so far away that we still see the light, but they could be dead already."

"You're right, that is crazy. You might just be a Zen lunatic after all."

"Oh yeah I asked you what that was early and you said you would tell me later. So what's a Zen Lunatic?" she asks.

"Well, Drew, Bear and I love philosophy, Asian religions like Buddhism and Taoism, and the Beat poets and writers of the mid-twentieth century, especially Jack Kerouac. Not so much his poetry, we prefer Ginsberg's poetry, but we love Jack's writing. On The Road and the Dharma Bums especially. In the Dharma Bums, Jack talks about the old Zen Lunatics of Asia and describes him and his friends as Zen Lunatics also, but he never really explains what a Zen Lunatic is. So we have spent many nights philosophizing about what a Zen Lunatic is. What we came up with was basically this, Zen is serenity, peace, patience, silence, meditation, etc. and a lunatic is the opposite, crazy, loud, wild, carefree, and spontaneous. It's yin and yang, positive and negative, opposites, it's a balance. You have to be both, you have to be Zen-like at times and a fucking lunatic at times, you can't be Zen all the time and you can't be a lunatic all the time, you have to be both. So we have adopted the Zen Lunatic way of life, we know how to chill and we know how to party, it's our way of life."

Caroline replies, "You're a trip, and that makes perfect

sense, I like it, I wanna be a Zen Lunatic."

"Well, you are on your way and I can help guide you on the Zen Lunatic path." I laugh. She laughs too as she takes the final hit of our joint. We are feeling good now as the drunkenness fades and the THC takes its place.

"I have to show you guys something tomorrow, it's a real Zen spot, you guys will love it," she says.

"Sounds like a plan." I turn my head, she turns hers and we are face to face. I take a chance and go in for a kiss. She meets me halfway and we kiss, under the stars or the holes to Heaven, which ever you believe, and it is perfect.

I slowly wake up to sounds coming from the kitchen. I am on the floor in the living room. I look over and see Rob and Tina cuddled up on the coach, still asleep. Drew is on the loveseat, alone, also asleep. Bear, Courtney, and Caroline are elsewhere. Caroline comes out of the kitchen and sees that I am awake.

"Coffee?" she asks.

"Yes please." My head feels pretty good but my body is scre as hell from sleeping on the floor. I rise and stretch, making loud stretching noises on purpose to wake up the rest of the gang. Courtney is the first to wake, then Rob. Drew is out cold so I walk over and gently kick him in the ass.

"Wake up Drew blew, we have shit to do." Drew moans and slowly begins to move and wake. I head to the kitchen and Caroline hands me a cup of coffee.

"If you want cream and sugar it's over there." she points to the counter by the oven and I head that way, I like lots of cream and lots of sugar.

"So where are we going?"

"You ever been up to see the Table Mountain wildflowers out by Oroville?"

"I heard about them when I was in college, but I never got up there."

"Well, that is where I wanted to take you guys if you have time?"

"We'll make time," I say, smiling.

Rob and Tina enter the kitchen and grab some coffee. I yell at Drew "hey Drew, you want some coffee?" He does and I take it to him. Rob, Tina, and Caroline come into the living room and sit down.

"Where the hell is Bear and Courtney?" I ask.

Rob answers, "In my room." He shakes his head.

"No shit? I didn't see that one comin'."

Drew gets up and walks towards Rob's bedroom. He opens the door and sees Bear's bare ass, Courtney has all of the covers.

"Wake up you crazy kids," Drew yells. Both Bear and Courtney jump up, rattled. Bear grabs one of his shoes and throws it at Drew hitting him in the left hip. Drew slams the door and returns to the living room.

"You're an asshole," I say, laughing.

"I was hoping to get a peek at Courtney's ass or tits, but all I got was Bear's ass burned into my brain, quick, Tina, let me see those titties?"

"I don't think so."

"Well, you can't blame a guy for tryin'."

We hear shuffling down the hall and I yell, "There is coffee in the kitchen." Bear yells back, "okay." Bear and Courtney each poor a cup of coffee and join us in the living room.

"Well, let's get ready and go," Caroline says.

"Where we goin'?" asks Bear as he takes a sip of his coffee.

"Caroline wants to take us up to Table Mountain to check out the wildflowers, it's supposed to be some real Zen meditative shit, which we need after our night of lunacy."

"Sounds good, but remember, we need to get to Seattle by tonight man," Bear adds.

"Yeah, I know, it's only ten hours or so to Seattle from here, we will be looking at the Space Needle by midnight."

"Alrighty then, let's get the show on the road," adds Drew.

We take a few minutes to get ready and head out the door. Courtney and Tina decided not to join us as they have already seen the wildflowers and had things to do. We get in the Jeep and head south on highway 99 towards Oroville. Thirty minutes later we pull into a small parking area and we can already see the wildflowers from the car. We get out and start our walk into the wildflower field. The colors are amazing, yellows and purples dominate the landscape with bits of orange, whites, and blues thrown in. It is a sea of colors and I see what Caroline meant when she said it was a Zen spot. There is not much talking as we walk among the wildflowers. It is like we are all alone, taking it all in, meditating on the beauty of this natural landscape. After about twenty minutes we head back to the car.

"You were right, that is a true Zen spot, you are on your way to becoming a Zen Lunatic," I whisper to Caroline.

She smiles and grabs my left hand, intertwining her fingers with mine. This has by far been the best twenty-four hours of my life. On our way back to Rob and Caroline's house we stop at a taco truck and grab a bag full of chicken and steak tacos. We get back to the house, eat, and pack up our things. We say our goodbye's and I tell Caroline that we will stop by on our way back to L.A, if that is cool. She says we better and kisses me. I smile and say "alright boys lets hit the road, Seattle is calling our names."

CHAPTER THREE

We head north out of Chico on Highway 99 and merge
onto Interstate 5 in Red bluff, which will take us all the way to
Seattle, which is about nine hours away. I am driving, like
always, Drew is shotgun, and Bear is in the back. As we make
our way north we drive through Redding and then up into the
mountains. We see Mount Shasta just to the northeast and as
we pass it we see an exit for the city of Weed and we have to
stop. As we exit Interstate 5 we see a sign that says Weed with
an arrow pointing right and underneath that it says College
with an arrow pointing to the left. We pull over, get out, and
take a picture of each of us under the sign holding our hands
up like which way should we go? We have already been to

college so we choose Weed, naturally.

We stop at a convenience store and there is all this merchandise that says weed on it, t-shirts, bumper stickers, shot glasses, etc. Bear spots a keychain that looks like a tiny California license plate and of course it says WEED on it, and of course we each buy one. We also grab some snacks and some road beers and jump back on Interstate 5, Seattle is now only seven hours north.

As we enter Oregon, Drew, now in the backseat, questions Bear, now shotgun, about his evening with Courtney.

"So Bear, give us the details man?"

"About what?"

"Don't play dumb, Courtney, last night, your bare ass in bed with her, ring a bell?" Drew interrogates.

"Oh, those details. A gentleman never tells." We all laugh, not because what he said was funny, but because we all know Bear is no gentleman.

I continue the inquisition, "Gentleman? Yeah right, just spill the beans man."

"Are you gonna tell us what happened on the roof Maximilian?" Bear tries to change the subject.

"What's to tell? We smoked a joint, looked at the stars, philosophized, kissed once, and went back inside."

"Come on Bear boy, give us the deets," Drew brings the discussion back to Bear and Courtney.

"Alright, you goddamn perverts," Bear gives in. "When you and Caroline went up on the roof the five of us finished our joints, as you already know Drew. Shortly after that Courtney whispered in my ear that she had something to show me and wanted me to follow her, which I did. She led me into a bedroom, which I assumed was Robs, because of the Pearl Jam poster on the wall and the dirty clothes on the floor. She shut the door behind me and told me to sit on the bed, which I did. She sat next to me and started shuffling through her purse. A few seconds later she pulls out a small baggy containing a white power that I assume is cocaine, which it was. She shakes the baggy and asks me if I have ever done it and I tell her once. I then begin to explain to her that the coke will kill our high and as she's pulling out a pocket mirror and a dollar bill she tells me she knows but she likes to fuck on blow."

Drew and I look at each other quickly, eyes wide, and I say "Damn, that's what I'm talkin' about." Drew nods his head and Bear continues.

"Yeah, no shit, so I tell her okay, fuck it, let's do it. She hands me the dollar bill and tells me to roll it up, which I do, as she pours a small amount of the coke on the mirror. She puts the baggy back in her purse and pulls out a business card which she uses to turn the small mound of coke into four three inch lines. I hand her the rolled up dollar bill and she explains to me that we each get two, one for each nostril. I nod my head and she tells me to hold the mirror, which I do. She puts the bill in her left nostril with her left hand, closes her right nostril with her right index finger, and snorts up one of the lines. Then she switches and snorts up another line into her right nostril. She hands the rolled up bill to me, takes a huge sniff, and shakes her head. I then hand her the mirror and I repeat what she just did. She takes the mirror from me, licks it, and then puts it back in her purse along with the dollar bill."

Drew interrupts, "she didn't lick the dollar bill?"

"No, you sick fuck, do you know how many people touch money, that's gross."

"Did you guys know that ninety percent of U.S. paper currency has some trace of cocaine on it?" I add.

"No shit?" Bear says.

"Ninety percent? That's bullshit," questions Drew.

"Look it up man."

"Hmm, anyway, Bear continue, and get to the good shit," Drew pushes.

"Well, after that we fucked, end of story."

"No, no, no, we want sex details, not drug use details, who cares if you did coke with this chick; tell us about the sex bro." Drew is getting irritated.

"Alright, but it's a short story if you know what I mean."

Drew, growing more impatient, "whatever man just tell it."

"Well, we start kissing and she grabs my package. She then violently pulls my shirt off and then starts unbuckling my belt. Then she pulls my pants off, without unbuttoning my pants. She then tells me to stand up, which I do with lightning speed. She stands up and takes off her clothes. She then gets on all fours on the edge of the bed, looks back at me, and says "what are you waiting for?" I'm flying now, the coke has kicked in and all of this chick's business is in my face. I don't even take my boxers off, I just pull my shit through the slit of my boxers and go to work. Shit, I still have my socks on. I'm like a jackrabbit going at it full speed. I'm a fuckin' jackhammer on high and literally sixty seconds later we finish, at the same time. Then we laid there for an hour talking about random shit until we fell asleep."

"Goddamn, that's awesome," Drew proclaims.

"Yeah, I second that," I add.

"So are you gonna fuck her again on our way back? Drew asks.

"I don't think so, I think that was a one and done deal. She didn't say a word to me in the morning or when she left, no goodbye, no number, no nothin'. But it's cool I don't care either way."

We reach Eugene two and a half hours later and flip off the exit sign for the University of Oregon, which we hate because we are huge USC Trojan fans and they are our arch nemesis. We cruise through Portland and cross the Washington state line about an hour and a half later. We are now only about two and a half hours away from Seattle. We reach the southern city limit of Seattle at eleven on the dot. We are supposed to meet Drew's buddy Big T at a house party when we get into town so we decide to just head there and see the Space Needle tomorrow.

We arrive at the house party twenty minutes later after passing it twice and trying to find a parking spot, parking in

Seattle is a bitch. We roll up to the front door and just walk inside. We walk into the kitchen looking for Big T and a drink. There are several bottles of liquor on the kitchen counter and a keg in the corner in a trashcan filled with ice. There is a stack of red plastic cups by the liquor bottles so we each grab one and pour ourselves a beer. Drew is on the keg pump, pumping away as I fill my cup with ice cold deliciousness. I take over for Drew and he and Bear fill their cups. At that moment Big T walks into the kitchen.

"Drew, my nigga." Big T yells, which he can say because he is a huge black man and no one will tell him he can't.

We all turn towards him. "Big T, what is up my brotha from anotha motha?" Drew yells.

It is so funny how Drew, and other people, act differently when they are around their black friends. They do a fist pound and a bro hug and Drew introduces us. We head into the living room and Big T introduces us to some of his buddies. We finish our beers, get a refill, and then head outside to smoke a cigarette and chat. The music inside is real loud and yelling over it is getting old. When we get outside there is already a half dozen people outside smoking. One of them is a gorgeous thin blond that Drew begins to chat with.

"Hey, how's it goin'?"

"Good, how are you?" she says in a sexy European accent.

"I'm good. I like your accent, where are you from?" Drew inquires.

"Guess." she says. We are all listening in and become part

of the conversation.

"Um, Russia?" answers Drew.

"Nope."

Bear gives it a shot, "the Ukraine?"

"Nope."

I give it a try, "The Czech Republic?"

"Yes, you are right, good job. Do you know where that is?" she asks.

"Central Europe." I answer.

"Yes, very good."

"I like geography." Bear, Drew, and Big T look at me like, you did not just say that to this hot ass chick?

"What? I do." I then realize how lame that was.

"Well if you think you are so smart I will ask you a question and if you can answer it I will give you a kiss, okay?" she says.

"Um, yeah, quiz me." I can see Drew is pissed because he got shut out last night and he was the one that started talking to this chick.

"What is the capital of the Czech Republic?"

"Hmm, that's a tough one." It wasn't really, I know the answer, but I wanted Drew to get the kiss.

"Let me think about that one for a second." I turn my head and slyly whisper to Drew "Prague." I tell her I don't know the answer but maybe one of my buddies does.

"Do any of you guys know the answer?" I ask.

Drew chimes in, "is it Prague?"

"Yes, very good." she leans over and gives Drew a kiss, on the cheek. He smiles and so does she. She goes back inside and Drew thanks me for the hook up, but is irritated that it was only a kiss on the cheek. I assure him that he will be hitting that by the end of the night. He tried for the next two hours but failed.

Around two in the morning we left the party, the four of us guys, no ladies. We are hungry so we stop for some Dick's, a local late night burger spot, not actual dicks. The place, which was famously mentioned in the Sir Mix-a-Lot song, *My Posse's on Broadway*, was the place to eat after the bars down by the University of Washington. Drew, Bear and I get in one of the five lines that are open, each one about five people deep. Big T stays behind in the car. While we are waiting in line Drew spots a hot chick that makes eye contact with him three lines down. As soon as he looks at her the guy she is with sees him looking at her.

"What are you looking at?" the guy yells.

"Her," Drew says pointing to the chick the guy is with.

The guy, who is white and about five foot five quickly walks towards us, pushing his way through the people in the other lines. We cannot believe he is doing this because he is alone, except for the girl, who stays in line, and there are three of us.

"What the fuck man?" the guy says about six inches from Drew's face. Bear and I are on each side Drew, ready to pounce.

"I was just looking at that beautiful woman over there."
Drew points at her. "Is that your girl?"

"No, she is my friend and I don't appreciate you looking at
her." The guy starts to get a little too close to Drew so I extend
my right arm and put it in between them. They go back and
forth a couple more times and I am real close to wrapping my
extended arm around this guy's neck and choking him the fuck
out, but none of us want to spend the night in jail and we were
really hungry. At that moment the guy walks back over to the
girl, who is about to order. He has no idea how lucky he was
that he left. We order, get our food, and head back to Big T's
car.

"Where the hell were you man?" Drew asks Big T.

"What are you talking about?"

"We almost had to kill a guy."

"Why?"

"Cause he didn't like me looking at his girl, that wasn't
even his girl."

"Shut the fuck up. You serious?"

"Yeah, what the hell were you doing? Jerkin' off?"

"No man, I was resting my eyes."

"That's cool man, it was three to one anyways; we had it
under control," I added.

We head back to Big T's place and just leave my Jeep at
the house party; we will get it tomorrow. At Big T's we drink
beers and smoke a blunt Big T rolled for us, Bear took notes.
We pass out around four in the morning, Big T had to work at

eight so he headed to bed around three.

Big T kicked us awake at noon. He was on his lunch break and told us to get up so he could take us to my Jeep before he had to go back to work. We slowly rise, put our shoes on and head out. Big T drops us off at my Jeep and we say our goodbyes. Big T drives off as we get into the Jeep.

"I need coffee," I say. Bear and Drew agree and we head to the nearest diner. After three cups of coffee each and some pancakes we head downtown to check out the Space Needle, the entire reason for this trip, but not really, I just wanted to get out of L.A for a little bit.

Parking downtown on a work day is insane, but I find a parking garage close by for five bucks an hour. We get out and head towards the Space Needle, which isn't as tall as I thought it would be. We walk up to the ticket window and about shit our pants, fifteen bucks for an elevator ride to the top? That is horseshit, but we came all this way, so fuck it. They know they can charge whatever they want because tourists like us come here to see this stupid thing and what are they going to do, come all this way and say no, we're not going to the top? Fuck no they won't, just like we didn't, fucking capitalism. We get our tickets, go inside, and get in line. Before you can even get on the elevator they make you take a picture with a fake Seattle skyline behind you, which we do, fucking capitalism, what the hell.

We get on the elevator and there is a tour guide guy who gives us a forty-five second fact rundown about the Space

Needle. He finishes his spiel just as the doors open, which is planned. We exit the elevator and head to the observation deck, which gives you a three-sixty view of Seattle, the Sound, and Mount Rainier, just like in the pictures I have seen. But this is a million times better. It is the Zen moment I thought it would be. You can see the entire sound to the west, Mount Rainier to the southwest, Lake Washington and Bellevue to the east, and possibly Canada to the North. It was the culmination of the entire trip.

I think back to the lunacy of the prank on Crazy J, the dancing at LaSalle's, and the almost murder at Dick's. I also think back to the Zen moments, lying on the roof with Caroline looking at the stars, walking amongst the wildflowers at Table Mountain, and standing here, atop the Space Needle, looking out at hundreds of miles of some of the greatest land America has to offer. It was perfect. And at that moment I thought of Caroline and was excited to leave Seattle and see her on our way home. But the journey home will have to start tomorrow because we have some more partying to do. The night cannot come any quicker.

After our Zen moment at the top of the Space Needle we hop back on the elevator and exit, through the gift shop of course, fucking capitalism. We decide to continue our tourist romp through Seattle and head down to Pike's Place Market which is only a few blocks away. Pike's Place Market is basically a farmer's market with some eating establishments and of course the first Starbuck's coffee shop, which we hit up first. I order the usual, a venti soy vanilla latte minus the whip cream. Drew orders his usual, a grande Americano and Bear orders his usual, a venti green tea soy latte. They taste the same here as everywhere else, which we figure, but we were hoping that since this was the holy land of coffee it would taste better, it didn't.

We walk through the market, window shopping as we go, until I spot the largest Fuji apples I have ever seen. I absolutely love Fuji apples and these are the size of softballs, so I buy two. We continue to walk through the market and finally end up at the famous Pike's Place Fish Market where an employee is throwing a large salmon from the crowd, through the counter, to another employee who catches it in a large sheet of paper and then wraps it up for the customer who purchased it. That is some serious Zen lunacy right there.

After the fish throw show we walk down an alley and see a clam chowder place and decide that we should probably get a bowl since we are in Seattle and this kind of shit is supposed to be fantastic here. We get our chowder and take a seat at a table just outside the place. There is a guy in his forties playing some classic Seattle grunge songs from the nineties on a beat up acoustic guitar across from us. He plays a Nirvana song and then an Alice in Chains song, both sound real good. The chowder is fantastic like we had hoped and we sit there quietly eating our chowder and listening to the sounds of our young adulthood. I notice the guy is selling CDs so after I finish my chowder and he finishes his current song, I walk over and ask him if those cover songs are on the CD. He says no that they are all originals. I tell him that he should have a CD of those grunge covers because they are really good. He says thanks and I walk back to our table after I throw a couple of bucks down in his opened guitar case.

We have had enough of the touristy bullshit, so we go back to the Jeep and try to find a cheap hotel for the night. We did not want to bother Big T because he had to work and we wanted to be closer to downtown anyway so we didn't have to drive. We find a room about five miles from Pioneer Square, which is the area of downtown Seattle that we want to party in tonight. It is only two in the afternoon and we are beat, so we decide to take a nap and recharge our batteries for the night ahead.

We awake six hours later, the longest nap ever, which is fine because it is eight now and we still have plenty of time until we have to head out. Bear leaves to explore the area for a place he can buy some beers and returns thirty minutes later with a twelve pack of Rainier, a locally made cheap beer that is surprisingly good. We chill in the room, drinking beers and talking. I am on one bed, Drew is on the other bed, and Bear is in one of the chairs by the window.

"So, what's up with you and that Caroline chick Mad Max?" Drew asks.

"I don't know man, she's cool as hell. That reminds me I have to call Rob and remind him that we will be stopping by for the night tomorrow." I grab my phone and call him. There is no answer so I leave a voicemail telling him that we should be by around ten tomorrow night and to let Caroline know. I hang up and Drew interrogates me some more.

"So you gonna bang her?"

"Don't plan on it, but whatever happens, happens man."

About fifteen minutes to ten we start getting ready. At ten, I call a cab and we head down to the lobby. The cab arrives, we jump in, and I tell the driver to take us to Pioneer Square. Ten minutes and thirty-five dollars later we arrive. I give the driver forty bucks and we get out. We walk a block and see a place called Cowgirls that is rockin' and we decide to check it out. When we get inside we head to the bar, where every bartender is a hot ass chick in cowboy boots, short denim skirts, and small cowgirl shirts that in no way cover their flat stomachs. We take a seat at the bar and order three Red Bull and vodkas. At different moments during the night the bartenders get up on the bar and do a little song and dance leaving every guy in the bar with their mouths wide open, including ours. We drink a little and dance a little, then we drink some more and dance some more. Before we know it, it is one-thirty in the morning, last call.

We leave the bar and search for some late night grub. We walk a couple blocks and find a hotdog stand. We order three dogs with cream cheese, which sounded interesting, and ate them quickly. They were surprisingly good. As we walked down the sidewalk we all of a sudden noticed that everyone around us is Black. We come to an intersection and a Black guy that was crossing the street cut in front of us, nudging Drew.

"What the fuck man?" Drew yelled.

The guy stopped and walked back towards us.

"What mothafucka?" the guy yelled back.

Drew got in his face. Bear and I notice all of the Black people around us staring and we pull Drew away.

"Its cool man, it's cool," I say to him.

"You better keep your bitch on a leash," he yelled.

We walk away and quickly cross the street.

"We better find a cab and get the hell out of here before we get killed," I suggest.

Bear agrees, but Drew is still pissed and starts cursing and yelling the N-word, which is surprising because he loves Black people. At that moment I wish Big T was with us. We tell Drew to shut the fuck up.

We finally spot a cab and jump in, we are safe, for now. I tell the driver which hotel we are staying at and we are on our way. A few block away I realize I do not have any cash to pay the cab driver. I tell him we need to find an ATM machine so we can pay him. He finds a bank and stops right in front of its ATM.

I open the door and say, way too loud, "let's go, let's bail, let's run."

"He can hear you man, just go get the money." Bear says. I look at the driver, smile, exit the cab, and head to the ATM. I return with two crisp twenty dollar bills and we are off to our final destination. We get to the hotel, I pay the driver with the two twenties, and we head up to the room. We smoke some weed out of an apple pipe Bear made from one of my giant Fuji apples, blowing the smoke out the window, and we fall asleep shortly after.

CHAPTER FOUR

We wake up to the sound of housekeeping knocking on the door yelling "housekeeping." I yell back, "No thank you." and she leaves. It is eleven-forty and we only have twenty minutes until we have to check out. We decide to just shower at Rob's so we throw our shoes on, grab our packs, and head down to the lobby. Ten minutes later we are on the road, southbound this time on Interstate 5. We get to Chico in record time, pushing the limits of my Jeep, and avoiding any money hungry highway patrol officers. We park in front of Rob and Caroline's house, get out, and head to the front door. Caroline opens the front door before we get there.

"It's about time," she says smiling.

I smile back, "We got here as fast as we could."

We enter the house and toss our bags in the same spot we did last time. Caroline gives me a big hug as Rob comes out from his bedroom.

"Mad Max and the road warriors. Damn, how long has it been?"

"Um, three days?" I say and we all laugh.

"So what's the plan?" Rob inquires.

"Well, we need to shower first and foremost, didn't get a chance to this morning, we woke up right before check out."

"I thought I smelled something." Caroline says playfully.

"Ha ha, but I do stink, no doubt."

"The shower is open, so help yourselves," Rob says. We all shower and put on clean clothes. Rob asks the question again.

"So what's the plan?"

"I was thinking we would stay in, drink a little wine, and maybe have a little poetry reading?"

"That sounds like a good plan. I can head to the store and grab some wine?" Rob offers.

"Perfect. Is all of this cool with you guys?" I ask. They all love the plan. I try to give Rob some cash for the wine but he won't take it. He leaves and we all fall into the couches to rest our weary bones before we have to party it up tonight.

Of the three of us Bear is the poet. Even though I have written many poems I am more of a writer, a more formal story teller. Drew is new to writing and poetry, but has a few good ones. Bear's poetry is more spiritual than mine. Mine are more social and political. Drew's stuff is mostly about his childhood and the beach. I am getting tired of the all the political and social poetry that I have written and I want to start focusing more on nature and love poems in the future. Caroline tells us that she has written a couple poems and wants to share them as long as we don't laugh. We tell her that we never laugh at poetry and that she should feel free to share if she wants. Rob returns twenty minutes later with two boxes of red Zenfandel, which is what I like to call it.

"Ah, just like college." I say.

Rob sets the two boxes of wine on the coffee table and leaves the living room. He returns with five plastic cups and passes them out.

"Okay, who's up first?" Caroline inquires.

"Well Bear is the poet laureate here, so he should go first," I suggest.

He agrees and asks Drew to grab his poetry notepad out of his pack. I ask him to grab mine too. Drew hands Bear his, hands me mine, and keeps his own. Caroline jumps up and runs out of the room.

"So you guys travel around with those in your packs?" Rob asks.

"Of course," I say.

"Always. You never know when a great poem will explode from your soul. You have to be prepared," Bear adds.

Caroline returns with two sheets of lined paper, which I

assume are the two poems she was talking about earlier.

Bear's first poem is one that I have not heard before. It is a short poem about Buddhism and true essence of enlightenment. I go next and read a social poem about the journey of life and how fucked up and boring it is. Drew follows me with a poem about his mother and how she raised him to be a good, respectful, young man and how he turned out to be a lunatic. Caroline is next and she is super nervous, but I tell her to just read it and that it will be fine.

"I wrote this after you guys left the other day," she explained.

She reads it and it is beautiful, a simple short poem about the wildflowers we visited three days ago. When she finished we all clapped, no snapping, that shit is stupid, and I tell her that it was beautiful. She tells me that she wants to take me back to the wildflowers tomorrow so she can show me something else that we did not have time to see last time. I tell her that I would love to.

"Rob Roy, do you have a poem you want to share?" Bear asks.

"No sir, I am just a casual observer and a fan, you four have it under control."

We finish the first box of wine and Rob opens the second. Bear starts into another poem, this one longer and more soulful than the last; this one I have heard before. The poetry reading goes on for an hour and we switch to conversations ranging from religion and philosophy to love, death, and sex.

We finish the second box of red zinfandel and Bear rolls two joints. We smoke them while we watch Jay and Silent Bob Strike Back, watching the Scooby Doo scene over and over and over again, laughing hysterically. Around two in the morning Caroline stands up, grabs my hand, and leads me to her bedroom. We do not make love, but we hold each other the entire night, and it is amazing.

I wake up alone in Caroline's bed. A few minutes later she walks in the room in my t-shirt holding two cups of coffee.

"Lots of cream, lots of sugar." she says, smiling, as she hands me a cup.

"You remembered, thank you."

"So are you ready for our little adventure?"

"I will be after this fine cup of coffee and maybe some breakfast."

"Of course, there is a great pancake place on the way."

We finish our coffee and get dressed. Caroline throws a couple of towels and a couple of bottles of water into her pack. The guys are still asleep in the living room as we head out the door. I almost go back inside to leave a note telling them where we are, but decide not to. We stop at a little diner just outside of town and enjoy some breakfast and more coffee. I order banana nut pancakes and she orders chocolate chip pancakes, complete with a whip cream smiley face. After our delicious breakfast we head to Table Mountain.

We park in the same spot and start down the path we walked down a few days ago. The colors are more vibrant this time, the purples and yellows exploding from the ground, as do the blues and whites. It is like we are walking through a painting. We get to the point on the trail where we turned around last time, but we continue on. We wrap around a canyon to the right and head down a ravine that didn't have a clear trail. We make our way out of the ravine and into the canyon. The rock walls around us are enormous grey structures that remind me of Devil's Postpile near Yosemite National Park. I went there on a YMCA trip when I was thirteen. I can hear what sounds like a waterfall not too far in the distance and sure enough as we make our way through a group of trees there it is, a beautiful waterfall which is at least a hundred feet high, possibly two.

"Well, what do you think?" she asks.

"It's amazing," I say, looking up admiring its beauty. "I assume you brought the towels because we're getting' in?

She takes off her shoes and socks. "Yep, but only if you want to," she says as she takes off her shirt exposing a blue string bikini top. My eyes get wide as she takes off her cut-off denim shorts exposing the matching blue string bikini bottom. She slowly gets in the water.

"It's cold, but you'll get used to it."

I say, "Okay" and I remove my shoes, socks, t-shirt, and shorts, exposing my blue plaid boxer shorts. I touch the water with my right big toe and she wasn't lying, it was freezing. But I slowly make my way into the water, which is only waist deep. Caroline is now screaming as she enters the waterfall and it covers her insanely fit body with freezing cold water. She comes out of it soaking wet, extends her right arm towards me, and calls me over with her index finger. I do not hesitate and quickly make my way over to her. We embrace and I scream as water from above sprinkles on me. She calls me a big baby and kisses me. The water is no longer cold, in fact I can't even feel it as I stare into her eyes.

We kiss again, a passionate kiss, the kind of kiss people dream and daydream about. It was as if we were characters in a romantic film based on a Nicholas Sparks novel. We move too close to the heart of the waterfall and the power of it forces us to end our kiss, way too soon. She takes my hand and leads me back to the bank. She grabs the two towels out of her pack and I extend my hand to take one but she does not offer me one. She lays them both down on the bank, removes her bikini top and then her bottoms, and lies down on the towels. She looks at me with wanting eyes, I remove my boxers, and lie down on top of her. We make love and it is like nothing I have ever experienced before.

When we finish, we lie there looking up at the waterfall that will forever be burned into our hearts and minds. It was the true meaning of Zen, total meditation, total serenity, and at that moment nothing else mattered. I could die at this moment and I would be perfectly okay with that. Not surprisingly, negative thoughts begin to enter my head and I suggest we go.

We head up the ravine and through the wildflowers, back to my Jeep. When we got back to the house the guys were in the living room watching television.

"Well there you two are." Rob says like a parent who waited up all night worrying about us.

"I was gonna leave a note but forgot to."

"No worries Mad Max."

"You ready to hit the road man? I have to go into work tomorrow or I will be fired." Drew asks.

"Yeah man, let's pack it up," I say as Caroline squeezes my hand, which tells me she doesn't want me to go.

I grab my pack and Caroline and I head to her room. As I pack, Caroline and I talk. We agree to keep in touch and we exchange numbers. I tell her that I will try to make my way back up here in a couple of months. She tells me that she plans on visiting her parents in San Diego this summer and will try to stop by on her way through L.A. We hug and kiss a final time and I leave her bedroom and head into the living room.

"You men ready for battle?" I ask.

"Sir, yes sir," yells Bear and Drew in unison.

"Well let's go."

We thank Rob for his hospitality and head out. We get on Highway 99 southbound and head home. Eight hours later we see the lights of Los Angeles and it is bittersweet. We are home, for now.

CHAPTER FIVE

It has been five months since the Seattle road trip when I receive a phone call from Rob. He asks me what is up between Caroline and I and I tell him that we have been calling and texting since I left last spring. I ask him why and he tells me that he thinks she might be seeing someone. My heart feels like someone stabbed it with a knife and my stomach hurts, I think I might puke, but I don't. I don't let Rob know how much it hurts and tell him that we are not together so she can do whatever she wants. He says okay, but I can tell he doesn't buy my "whatever" attitude about it. He suggest I call her to see what is up and I agree. This explains the tapering off of the calls and texts over the last month.

I pick up my phone and give Caroline a call. She answers and we talk. I ask her what is going on and that I have noticed that our calls and texts have been few and far between over the past month or so. I tell her to just be honest with me. She comes clean and tells me that she met a guy a month ago on the first day of school. He is in the teaching program with her. They sat next to each other and had to introduce one another and they just hit it off. She says that she planned on telling me but just didn't know how to. I tell her its fine (I lie) and that we are not together so she can do whatever she wants. I also express that I am happy for her and I wish her well (I lie again). She seems confused by what I say, probably not expecting that reaction, and simply says okay. I tell her I have to go and I hang up, without saying goodbye. At that moment there is a knock on my bedroom door and I tell whoever it is to come on in.

The door opens and it is Bear, his hair now short and he is sporting a new moustache. Yes a moustache. He never told us until recently but he was totally enamored with Crazy J's handlebar moustache when we picked him up on our way up to Seattle. The stache fit him though and we agreed to let him keep it, reminding ourselves that your outer appearance does not make you a Zen Lunatic, your actions do, and Bear was still the same old Zen Lunatic he had always been.

"What's going on Mad Max?" Bear and Drew have started to call me that ever since they heard Rob call me that in Chico.

"Caroline is seeing somebody."

"Shit, I'm sorry man that sucks."

"Yeah well what did I expect? She lives in Chico, I live in L.A."

"Yeah, but you told me your plan was to keep in touch with her and hope that when she finishes school she would take a teaching job here and you two could..."

I interrupt, "Fuck it man, shit happens for a reason, right?"

"Yeah, it does."

"You got any plans this week?" I ask.

"Not really, what's on your mind?"

"I think it's time to get out of town again, before winter comes. I have had a road trip planned for years and I think this is the perfect time to do it."

"Oh yeah, what's the plan?

"Utah."

"Utah?" Bear inquires.

"Yep, Zion, Bryce, Arches, Canyonlands, Bridges, Monument Valley, and the Grand Canyon. A fuckin' Zen romp through the most beautiful lands in the west and possibly the world. With a stop in Vegas of course, you know since it's on the way."

"I'm down, but on one condition."

"Sure man, what is it?"

"We stop in Phoenix on the way back, I have some friends there I want you to meet."

"Of course. Leave tomorrow?"

"Sounds good to me." Bear shuts the door and I am left

alone, lying on my bed, thinking about Caroline.

The next morning Bear and I pack up and head out. Drew can't make the trip because he can't get the time off from work. We hop on Interstate 10 east out of Los Angeles and then merge onto Interstate 15 north, which will take us all the way to Vegas. We stop in Barstow for lunch and gas and then head back onto interstate 15 northbound, we are only two hours from Vegas.

"So you want to talk about this Caroline situation?" Bear asks.

"Nah, I just want to forget about that for a while. Let's just go crazy and try to learn a little about ourselves in the process."

"So the usual?"

I smile and chuckle, "yeah, the usual."

We come up over the final hill as the sun begins to set and we see the beautiful Las Vegas landscape. A city in the middle of the desert, built up over the decades, the Devil's playground, where people go to live and die. We pull into the parking lot of the Tropicana Hotel where we will be staying for the night. It is not as glamorous at some of the other hotels but its location is perfect. Across the street to the north is the Excalibur and next to that to the west is the Luxor. To the East is the MGM Grand and caddy corner, or kitty corner depending on where you are from, is the New York New York, my favorite.

We check in and head to our room. The room is your basic

two queen bed room with a television and a table with two chairs. Which is fine because we do not plan on spending too much time in the room. We throw our packs on the beds and head down to the casino floor to find a place to eat.

When we get down to the casino Bear says he has to use the bathroom, so I take a seat in front of a dollar slot machine and wait for him. About a minute later a guy walks up to me and asks if I am using the machine. I say no and he asks if he can use it. I look around and every machine is open within fifty feet of us, but I say "sure" and get up. Bear exits the bathroom and I start to walk towards him when I hear a siren go off behind me. I turn around and the slot machine that I was just at, which that guy is now at, was flashing its lights and making a loud obnoxious noise.

"No fucking way," I say.

"What?" Bear asks.

I take a couple of steps towards the machine and see that the guy, on his first pull of the lever, won four hundred dollars. I walk back over to Bear shaking my head.

"What happened man?"

"I was sitting at that machine, waiting for you, and that guys wanted that machine so I got up and he just won four hundred bucks, what the fuck!"

"Unreal," Bear says.

"Yeah, no shit. Let's gets some food before I kill that guy or myself."

We eat at the Island Buffet, a typical Las Vegas buffet, and it is not too bad. We fill our bellies to capacity so we don't get too drunk, too fast tonight. We spend some time, and money, at the Tropicana casino, playing video poker at a bar and throwing back a couple of beers. We decide to head back up to the room to shower and change and relax a bit before the long night ahead. It is a Monday night, but this is Vegas, and every night in Vegas is a long night. Besides, the night is how you make it.

At ten o'clock we get ready to hit the town. We start out at the MGM Grand Hotel and take a seat at a five dollar blackjack table that has two open seats. We win a few hands and loose a few hands. A waitress in a scantily clad outfit approaches our table and asks if anyone needs a cocktail. Bear and I order a couple Red Bull and vodkas and continue playing. Five minutes later she returns with our drinks, free of course, but I tip her a five dollar chip and I tell her to bring us another round when she can. I have been to Vegas enough to know that if you tip big at first, the drinks will come quicker. After paying sixty bucks for four drinks, we lost fifty at the table and ten in tips, we get up and decide to make our way over the bridge to the New York New York Hotel.

We enter the New York New York and run into the Coyote Ugly Bar. We order a couple beers and stand next to the dance floor to survey the scenery, which means looking for hot chicks to hit on. I see two sevens, one blonde, one brunette, standing together about ten feet to the right of us and I suggest we give it a shot. Bear agrees and asks what our story is.

Every time we go to Vegas we have a story about what we do for work. I suggest we tell them we are ad executives, because the Hollywood producer and the, we are in a band thing, is played out. He agrees and we walk over.

"How's it goin'?" I ask them.

The blonde replies "good, how are you guys doin'?

"Life is good, can't complain," I answer.

"So where are you ladies from?" Bear inquires.

"Denver. Where are you guys from?" The blonde asks.

"L.A," I say.

The brunette chimes in, "let me guess, you guys are movie producers, right?"

Bear and I look and each other and laugh. "No, I take it you get that a lot?" I ask.

"Twice already tonight," the brunette replies.

"Guys are idiots," Bear says.

"Yeah, no, we are not movie producers, we are ad execs," I say.

"What?" the blonde asks, the music is loud and it is a little hard to hear.

I repeat, "We're advertisement executives, you know TV commercials."

"Oh, you guys make TV commercials?" the blonde asks.

"Well, we don't actually make them, we basically come up with ideas for TV commercials, and then companies buy those ideas and they make the commercials." I am totally making this shit up, I have no idea what an ad executive does or if it is even a real job, but these chicks don't know.

"Is there a commercial that we've seen that you guys came up with?" the brunette asks.

I continue the bullshit. "Well, the only one that went national was a Superbowl spot we came up with that was purchased by Pepsi."

"Which one was that?" the brunette asks, still skeptical.

"It was the Pepsi Twist one where Ozzy Osborne's kids turn into the Osmond's." I pull that one out of my ass.

"I remember that one," the blonde exclaims. The brunette does not look convinced and tells her blonde friend that she needs to use the restroom and asks her to go with her, which she does.

"Do you think they bought it?" I ask Bear.

"What do you think?"

"I think the blonde did." We bust out laughing.

"They're not comin' back man," Bear says.

"Yeah, I know, but fuck it, the night is young and I'm not gonna trip on a couple of sevens." We bust out laughing again.

Bear adds, "You had me convinced though, with the whole commercial thing, well done."

"A thank you sir." We finish our beers and head to my favorite bar in the place, which is right in the middle of the casino, the Bar at Times Square, a dueling piano bar.

It is almost midnight when we get to the Bar at Times Square. We pay the ten dollar cover and walk in. The pianos are dueling away to Billy Joel's *Piano Man*, which is no surprise, since it is a crowd favorite. We get to the bar and have to yell our drink order because the entire place is singing along and it is loud. We both order beers and they come quickly. We turn around and survey the scene, same as we did at Coyote Ugly. This is what we do when we go to any bar, it is our modus operandi. We don't see much so we just stand there drinking beers and singing along to classics like Christopher Cross's *Sailing Away*, Bon Jovi's *Living on a Prayer*, and of course Elton John's *Benny and the Jets*. About twenty minutes pass and in my right ear I hear a woman's voice.

"Hi."

I turn my head towards the voice and lock eyes with a cute, dark haired chick. "Hey. How are you?" I say as I nudge Bear with my left elbow to get his attention to the situation.

"I'm good, so what's your name?"

"I'm Max." I extend my right hand and she shakes it. "What's your name?" I ask still shaking her hand.

"Delilah and this is my friend Rachel." she points to her friend that is standing to her right sipping on an apple martini. I shake her hand.

I put my left arm around Bear's neck and introduce him, "This is my buddy Bear." He shakes both of their hands.

"Bear? Is that a nickname?" asks Delilah.

"It's short for Barry," I answer.

"And Max is short for Mad Max," Bear interjects and we laugh.

"So, are you mad?" Delilah inquires.

"Well..."

Bear interrupts, with a country accent, "Mad Max is the craziest sumbitch this side of the Mississippi." We all laugh. Bear has clearly had too much to drink.

"So you ladies need another drink?"

Delilah answers, "We would love one, two apple martinis please."

I tell Bear to order two apple martinis, two beers, and four chocolate cake shots, which he does.

"So, where are you ladies from?"

"Chicago, you guys?"

"L.A."

"What do you do in L.A?"

I decide not to lie and tell her the truth, well sort of. "I'm a writer. What do you do in the windy city?"

"I'm a legal assistant for a small law firm." she says. I have never fucked a lawyer before, this should be fun.

"What do you write?"

This is where I decide to lie. "I write TV screenplays."

Her eyes get real big. "Really? Like TV shows?"

"Yes, TV shows."

"Which shows?"

"I've written for *The Shield*, *Monk*, and *CSI*. Mostly crime dramas." I say this because I figure since she is in the legal field this will really wet her panties.

"I love those shows," she yells.

I was right.

Bear hands the ladies their shot, then hands me one, and then grabs his.

"What are these?" Rachel asks.

"Chocolate cake shots, they're good, trust me, it looks like water, but it tastes just like chocolate cake."

We lift our glasses and I say "here's to a great night." We take the shot and the ladies are surprised at how good they are.

"Yum," Delilah says. Rachel agrees with her evaluation.

Bear hands the ladies their apple martinis and he hands me a beer. I clank beers with Bear and we nod at each other as to say, here we go.

We drink and sing and talk for about thirty more minutes before I suggest to the ladies that we head to the Luxor for a change of scenery. They agree and we make our way across the bridge to the Excalibur Hotel and catch the tram to the Luxor. We are all hammered by now. Delilah has to use the restroom as soon as we get inside the Luxor. Bear and Rachel take a seat on the edge of a fountain pool to wait. I am standing about ten feet away when two guys walk by. Bear is offended that they would walk in between us, which is ridiculous, but he is drunk, and he yells at them.

"What the fuck bro?" he says.

One of the guys stops prompting his friend to stop also. He walks over to Bear and gets in his face.

"What motherfucker?" The guy says.

"What the fuck are you doing walking in between us like

that man?"

The guy looks at me as I make my way over and says, "he was way over there man." He was right but I start to get pissed off, just because I can.

I tell the guys buddy that he better get his friend out of here before he gets hurt, which is what I say every time I am in this situation, because it works, I am not a small guy. The friend looks at me, walks over to his buddy who is still yelling at Bear, and tells him to forget about it and that they should just leave, which they do. Bear looks at me and smiles.

"You fucktard, you trying to get us arrested?" I say. We both laugh as Rachel shakes her head, and Delilah walks up.

"What's so funny?" Delilah asks.

"Oh nothing, we just almost got into a brawl with a couple of Guidos," I say. Delilah looks at Rachel who is still shaking her head.

I add, "We should probably head back to the Excalibur before security comes."

We all agree, but now Rachel has to use the bathroom. I tell Bear that Delilah and I are going to head over to the Excalibur and that he should wait for Rachel and then meet us over there. He agrees and we head to the tram. We enter the tram thinking that it would be empty, but it is not, there is a guy sitting down next to three kids. This throws me off guard since it is almost three in the morning. The doors closes and Delilah decides to use the pole in the tram as a stripper pole. She is spinning around it and I look at the guy and shrug my shoulders. She continues as the tram comes to a stop.

I look at the kids and say "don't drink or do drugs or you'll end up like this." pointing at Delilah, who is not offended. We exit the tram and Delilah jumps on my back. I did not expect it and I fall forward bashing her head into a soda vending machine. We are now on the ground, laughing hysterically, Delilah is rubbing her head. We stand up about five minutes later just as Bear and Rachel exit the next tram. Rachel tells Delilah that she needs to talk to her and they walk off. Bear walks over and tells me that he has a story to tell me and I tell him that I have a story myself. He tells me to go first and I tell him about the guy and the kids on the tram and Delilah swinging around the pole, and her hitting her head. He laughs and then tells me his story.

"So I was waiting for Rachel and two hookers walked up to me and said that I could have both of them for three hundred bucks. I told them no, that I was good. Then one of them grabbed my dick and said "are you sure?" I pulled away and said no again and that I was good. Well they both got pissed off and started yelling at me as they stormed off. Then Rachel came back and we hopped on the tram. Then before the doors could close the two hookers got on the tram and sat directly across from us."

"No shit," I interrupt.

"I'm totally serious. So then the two hooker's just stare at me with pissed off looks on their faces. Now remember, Rachel has no idea what happened with these chicks while she was in the bathroom."

"Holy shit."

"Yeah, but wait there's more. So the tram starts moving and the hookers start yelling at me again. I looked at Rachel and she was like, what the fuck is this all about. I just shrugged my shoulders and just took the verbal abuse until the tram stopped and we jumped out."

At this point I was rolling, laughing so hard it hurt.

Delilah walks back over to us and tells us that Rachel has gone back to their hotel room. I assume that since she did not say that she was going with her that she wanted to go back to our room. I was correct in that assumption. We get back to the room and Bear passes out in one bed while I lay on the other. Delilah heads to the bathroom and then to my bed. We make out for a few minutes but nothing is going on in my pants. She proceeds to take my pants off, then my shirt. I take her shirt off and then her pants. Still nothing is happening downstairs. She takes my boxers off and I take her panties and bra off. Still no movement from my bald friend down below. She grabs my dick and notices that I am not hard so she tries to help me out. Still nothing. After about ten minutes of me trying to stick my limp noodle inside of her we give up. I have only had limp dick twice in my life and I am pissed. We pass out and I wake up several hours later alone. I start laughing hysterically, which wakes Bear up.

"Dude, what the fuck is so funny?" he asks, trying to sleep.

"I will tell you later bro."

We get up an hour later, pack up and check out. We grab some breakfast and I tell him what happened in the room last night. He laughed so loud everyone in the place was staring at us.

"That must have been some walk of shame for her," Bear says, laughing again.

I laugh with him and say, "at least she has a great story to tell all her friends. Hey remember that time we went to Vegas and I tried to sleep with that limp dicked loser?"

Bear adds, "I don't know if she will tell anyone that story."

"Why not?"

"She couldn't get you hard bro. No chick is gonna admit that she couldn't get a guy hard."

"True."

We finish eating, head to the jeep, jump on interstate 15, and head northeast towards Utah and our first stop, Zion National Park.

CHAPTER SIX

We make a pit stop two hours later in St. George, Utah for drinks and snacks that will fuel us for the next two days. The plan is to camp out at Zion National Park tonight and then Bryce Canyon National Park tomorrow night. I also decide to top off the gas tank so we don't have to worry about gas until we reach Moab, Utah in a couple of days. As we are about to take off, Bear notices a hitchhiker by the road in front of the gas station and asks if we should take him with us. I laugh and say no, besides we are only an hour away from our destination. We jump back on Interstate 15 and ten minutes later we merge right onto Highway 9. We drive through the tiny towns of Hurricane, La Verkin, Virgin, Rockville, and

Spr_ngdale.

North of Springdale we take a left onto Floor of the Valley Road and head straight north six miles to a parking lot at the end of the road, a sign there reads Temple of Sinawava. Our plan is to park here, hike the Narrows Trail, find a place to sleep, and hike back to the Jeep in the morning. We never like staying at campgrounds, because we want to experience nature's beauty in its rawest form. No tents, no stoves, just sleeping bags, the stars, the moon, the sounds of nature, and good philosophical conversation. That is our way. We got crazy last night in Vegas and now it is time to balance ourselves out and tap into the peaceful side of life. We exit the Jeep, Bear grabs the snacks and waters and we head to the back to grab our packs. I throw the snacks into my pack and Bear throws the waters into his. I close the back of the Jeep and we begin our hike north through the Narrows on a paved trail.

About a mile into our hike the paved trail ends and the trail turns to water, as in the north fork of the Virgin River. We continue on, up river, struggling a bit though the knee deep waters as the rocky bottom makes it hard to maintain balance. The tan and grey canyon walls shoot straight up to the blue sky above, shadowing us from the sun. They don't call this the Narrows for nothing. As we make our way upstream the canyon walls begin to creep up on us from both sides.

The water feels great. It is September and the weather is warm and amazing. We reach Orderville Canyon, which forks to the right, a mile and a half upstream. We decided to continue up the main canyon. As we make our way north the trail widens a bit and the sun hits us, warming our skin as well as our souls. We reach Big Springs about five miles into the hike. The sun is going down and most of the people we have seen have already headed back to their cars. After soaking in Big Springs we hike back a little ways to the wider area of the trail that we noticed before. We hike up the side until we reach a flat area that we call home for the night.

We unpack our sleeping bags, mats, and small pillows and lay them out. We sit down and I sift through my pack searching for our snacks. I find a bag of trail mix and pull it out. Bear grabs two bottles of water from his pack and hands one to me. I open the bag of trail mix and hand it to Bear, who takes a handful and tosses some into his mouth. I open my water and take a drink. Bear gives the trail mix back to me and I pour some into my mouth as Bear opens his water and takes a drink. We take off our wet shoes and socks and set them to the side.

"Great hike huh?" I say.

"Amazing man."

"I didn't expect to have to hike through the river like that though," I say.

"Yeah, but it felt nice. Except for the rocks."

"True, I almost fell in a few times, glad I didn't, would've been a cold bitch tonight."

It quickly begins to get dark as we snack on some more

trail mix and finish our waters. The temperature has dropped but it is still in the seventies. I lay down on my sleeping bag and mat and rest my head on my small camping pillow. Bear grabs something out of his pack, sets his pack to the side, and lays down on his sleeping bag. He thumbs his lighter, lights a joint, takes a hit, and passes it to me. I take a hit and pass it back to him.

"Damn, there's a ton of stars up there man," I say.

"Just as many as when you looked up there last time Max."

"Yeah, I know, but you can't see as many with those damn city lights blaring."

Bear takes another hit and passes it back to me and I do the same. "Hey Max, you ever think about leaving the city?"

"L.A? Sometimes. You?"

"Sometimes."

I add, "Sometimes I think about packin' up and movin' to Montana or Idaho or even Wyoming. Find me a little cabin in the woods, maybe on the bank of a lake or river. And I would just write and explore and write some more. And at night I would drink beers and smoke weed and just chill."

"That sounds awesome man. What's holding you back?"

"It's just not time yet. And I'm not sure if I want to go alone, or with a women, or try to convince one or both of you fuckers to go. I still have to figure out what I want out of life man."

"Yeah, I hear ya. I would go you know."

"Yeah, I know."

It is starting to cool down a bit more so we climb into our sleeping bags and we are in heaven, content, tired, and high.

"So, do you ever think about getting married Bear?"

"Married? Me? Not really. I don't think I could handle being with one women for the rest of my life. You?"

"Once in a while I think about it. I think it would be nice to share experiences with someone."

"Um, we share experiences all the time Max."

"You know what I mean, it's different with a chick. Remember when we were in Chico, on our way back to L.A and I left with Caroline to go check out the wildflowers again?"

"Yeah."

"Well we walked through the wildflowers and then down a ravine to a waterfall. It was one of the most beautiful things I had ever seen. Caroline and I kissed under that waterfall and then we made love on the bank."

"No shit?"

"Yep, and when we were done we laid there for a bit and I was staring up at that waterfall while she held me, eyes closed. And you know what I was thinking as I laid there?

"Nah man, what?"

"I was thinking, I don't deserve this. I didn't deserve her and I didn't deserve what I had just experienced."

"Why not?"

"That's the thing man, I don't know why. I pushed her away. I could have gone up there to see her. I could have told her how I really felt about her and how much I want to be with her. But I didn't, because for some reason I don't think I deserve her."

"Maybe the answer is in what you said a few minutes ago. Maybe it's just not the right time yet? Maybe you guys aren't meant to be together right now. But that doesn't mean you aren't meant to be together or that you don't deserve each other."

"This is why I keep you around Bear. That makes a lot of sense. And you're right, I'm not ready, but if I don't get ready soon, I might miss out on something special."

"Whatever you do, you're gonna miss out on something."

Bear is a genius, a fucking poet, and my best friend and as I lie there staring at the stars, I honestly believed that Caroline is on her roof staring at them with me. We chat for a little while longer and then pass out, early for us, but we are exhausted.

We awake to the sounds of hikers coming up the trail. We pack up our sleeping bags, mats, and pillows, throw on our packs and head back down to the trail. We hike the five miles back to the Jeep quickly and make our way back to Highway 9. Bryce Canyon National Park is only two hours away and we have some more hiking to do so I step on it. I blaze down the winding highway, making Bear wish he was back on the beach in L.A. He is holding on tight to the "oh shit" handle as I take turn after turn, yelling wildly, like a maniac being chased by the law.

We reach Highway 89 in record time and take a left and head north. Forty minutes later we hit Highway 12 and head east. Fifteen minutes after that we reach the Bryce Canyon Airport and take a right, heading south on Highway 63 for a short three mile drive to Fairyland Point Road. I take a left and a mile down the road we reach the Fairyland Loop Trailhead parking lot. We exit the Jeep and it is like we have, pardon the expression, died and gone to Heaven. It is one of the most beautiful landscapes we have ever seen. We look at each other in awe and look back towards the canyon, soaking in one of nature's finest works of art.

I pull out the trail map that was given to us at the entrance and look at it to figure out which direction we should head on the trail and where we should camp. After a short analysis, I conclude that we should start the trail to the right because the steeper parts that way are downhill and it will be a little easier. I tell Bear that we can finish the Loop by sunset and then sneak out onto Boat Mesa and sleep under the stars. He agrees with my evaluation of the situation and suggests we grab our packs and head out on the trail so we can make the loop by sunset. We don't want to be out on the trail after dark. Even though we have head lamps hiking at night sucks.

We start the hike and spend the first two and a half miles walking along the rim section of the trail. The view is insane. We reach Sunset Point and then take a sharp left and begin our descent into Campbell Canyon. The elevation drops eight hundred feet during the one and a half mile descent. We pass the China Wall, which is a beautiful grouping of hoodoos, which are tall, orange-ish tan, rock formations that were created by wind and rain erosion over millions of years. They shoot up towards the clear blue sky and are the major feature of Bryce Canyon National Park. They remind me of the Thunder Mountain Railroad roller coaster ride at Disneyland.

The sun is beating down on us making it seem a little warmer than it is. But the weather is perfect and the temperature is just like home, about seventy five degrees. A short time later we take a side trail to the right which leads to the Tower Bridge rock feature, named so because it looks a like the Tower Bridge in London. When we reach the end of the short side trail, I quickly notice two chicks sitting on a couple of logs sharing a snack. I nudge Bear and nod my head toward them.

Bear examines the scenery and says, "Looks good to me, what's the plan?"

"Picture time?" I say, holding up my phone.

"Yeah, I think we need someone to take a picture of us in front of this amazing natural wonder," Bear says.

"I totally agree, but who is gonna take the picture?" We both laugh, too loud apparently, as the two chicks hear us and look our way.

As we approach them I say, "Excuse me ladies, we were wondering if one of you could take a picture of us in front of this bridge thing?"

"Yeah sure, I can do it," says the short-haired chick as she stands up.

I hand her my phone, Bear and I walk a few steps, turn around, and I jump on Bear's back. The chicks laugh, we smile, and she takes the picture. I jump off Bear's back, walk back over, take my phone back and thank her. She says, "You're welcome" and walks back over to rejoin her friend.

We follow. "So where are you ladies from?" I ask.

They look at each other, smile, and the long-haired chick answers, "San Diego."

"Ah, nice. We're from L.A," I say.

"Cool," The long-haired chick replies.

"My name is Max by the way…" I put my hand on my chest. "…and this is my friend Bear." I shoot my thumb towards him.

"Bear?" the short-haired chick says.

"Short for Barry," he says.

"Bear is way cooler," I add.

"It is," the long-haired chick says.

We nod our heads and then wait, hoping they will tell us their names, which they do after a few moments of uncomfortable silence.

"Well, I'm Lacey and this is Jen," the short-haired chick says. They both extend their right hands and we shake both of them.

"Well we're gonna get back on the trail so we can finish before sunset," I say.

"Okay," Lacey says.

Bear looks at me confused and I nod for us to leave. We take a few steps, but I stop, turn around, and walk back, Bear follows.

"Hey." They look at me. "We're gonna sneak out onto Boat Mesa at dark and camp under the stars. If you two want to join us, we will be in the parking lot in a couple hours. Just wanted to throw that out there." I smile, we turn around, and we head back to the main trail. Bear is impressed, as he always is, with my ability to pick up chicks and I tell him that I fail more than I succeed, which he already knows.

As we make our way through the canyon we come to a point where we can see the Sinking Ship Mesa, which is a little ways beyond the canyon. It kind of looks like a sinking ship but not really. We make our way back to the trailhead and finish the loop in just under five hours. As soon as we see the parking lot we start looking for the chicks, just in case they were going the opposite direction that we went and finished before us, but they were nowhere to be seen. A half hour later the sun sets and we give up looking for them. I told Bear that they probably laughed at what I had said when we left and that they probably just headed out. I was wrong, because not two minutes later, Lacey and Jen walk up with their packs, and Lacey asked, "So what's the plan?"

I smile and tell them that we need to head back down the trail to the right. Then we need to jump off the trail to the left and head onto Boat Mesa without getting caught. They like the plan. Bear grabs his pack and I grab mine. The four of us head back down the trail and then jump off the trail and head onto Boat Mesa. We walk about a quarter mile and find a flat, somewhat open spot to set up shop. We lay out our sleeping bags, pads, and pillows. We all lie down and relax for a few minutes.

"Do you guys want some wine?" Jen asks.

"Um, yes. Do you have some?" I inquire.

"Yep, right here." She lifts up a Camelback pack.

"There's wine in there?" asks Bear.

"Sure is," she says as she puts the tube in here mouth and sucks some wine out of the bladder inside of the pack. She passes the pack to Lacey who takes a drink. Lacey passes the pack to me.

"And you don't care if I put my mouth on this?" I ask, holding the tube in front of my mouth.

"Do you care that our mouths were on it?" Jen asks.

"Not at all."

"Well, then we don't care." Jen smiles and I take a drink.

It's a red, and I am not a wino, but it taste like a cabernet. I don't ask what it is because I really don't care, its wine, and it tastes good. I pass the pack to Bear, he takes a pull off of the tube, and tosses the pack back over to Jen. We pass the pack around two more times. The high altitude assists us in our intoxication. Bear lightly kicks me, I look at him and he puts the thumb and index finger of his right hand to his lips simulating him smoking a joint. I nod my head as to say, yes that is a great idea. Bear shuffles through his pack and pulls out a joint and his lighter. The moon is almost full and gives us enough light to see pretty well.

"So, do you ladies smoke?" Bear asks, holding up a joint in front of him.

Jen replies, "I have, but it's been a while."

"I've never tried it," Lacey adds.

"Well, if you want to try it again." he points the joint towards Jen. "And you want to try it for the first time." he points it towards Lacey. "Then feel free." Bear lights the joint, takes a hit, and passes it to me. I do the same and hold it out towards Lacey who hesitantly and gingerly takes the joint from me with her thumb and index finger. She puts it between her big, beautiful lips and takes a hit, coughing almost immediately. We all laugh, but not very loud.

"Hey, it's my first time, be nice," she says.

We apologize as she passes the joint to Jen, who takes a hit like she has done it before. Bear tells her to take another and then pass it back around. She does and then passes it back to Lacey. I tell her to inhale it into her mouth only and then inhale it into her lungs, she does what I say and does not cough. She exhales the smoke, looks at me, and smiles.

"I did it," she exclaims, like she just road a bike without training wheels for the first time.

"Good job. Now pass it over here." I smile, take the joint, take a hit, and pass it to Bear. He finishes off the small joint and puts it out.

The wine and the weed have kicked in and we are feeling

great. The weather has cooled a bit so we climb into our sleeping bags and look up at the stars.

"So are you guys headed back to L.A tomorrow?" Lacey asks.

"Nope, we are headed to Moab tomorrow and then down to Monument Valley and the Grand Canyon. Then on to Phoenix for a couple of days and then back home to L.A." I answer.

"Wow, that's a nice little adventure," Jen says.

"Yes it is. Are you two headed back tomorrow?"

"Yeah, we need to get back, we have work," Jen answers.

"What do you ladies do?" Bear asks.

"Well, I'm a hairstylist and Lacey is a massage therapist. What do you guys do?"

"We're full time Zen Lunatics," proclaims Bear. I laugh and notice the ladies look confused.

"It's just our philosophical way of life, don't worry about it. I'm actually a writer and Bear sells medicinal marijuana."

"That's cool, I have never met a writer before. What do you write?" Lacey asks.

"Oh, a bunch of different things, short stories, poetry, things like that. I actually wrote a screenplay and I'm planning on starting my first novel soon."

"That's so cool."

We continue to talk for an hour longer, mostly about our jobs and our future aspirations. We fall asleep one by one under the light of a billion stars and one huge moon in one of the most beautiful canyons on earth. A great end to a great day.

The sun comes up over the horizon to the east and wakes me. I slowly sit up, look around, and notice everyone else still asleep. I look at the sun and then close my eyes and smile, the perfect Zen moment, which is shortly interrupted by Bear.

"What are you smiling at Mad Max?"

I open my eyes and look at Bear. "Everything man, the sun, this canyon, this moment, this life." I look back at the sun. "This is perfect, right here, right now. No worries, no bills, no traffic, no nothin'."

"Yeah, I feel ya. But there's one thing missin'?"

"Drew?"

Bear chuckles, "Well that's a given, but I was thinkin' about something else."

"What?"

"Tito's Tacos," he says with a look of ecstasy on his face.

"You dick. You had to say that didn't you? God, what I wouldn't do for a meat and cheese burrito right now." My stomach grumbles at the thought. We sit and stare at the wonders around us, waiting for Lacey and Jen to awake, which they do about twenty minutes later. We all pack up and head back to our vehicles. I make sure that I exchange numbers with both of them and tell them that I will give them a call sometime and maybe we can get together in San Diego in the near future. They agree and we head off to the north and the east, to Moab, which is four hours away.

We make our way back to Highway 89 and head north.

About an hour and a half later Highway 89 turns into Interstate 70 and then turns east. We are starving, but we decide to wait and eat when we get to Moab, We snack on the rest of our trail mix, which tides us over. Two hours later we reach the turn off for Moab and head south on Highway 191. Twenty minutes later we pass Arches National Park and roll into Moab. It is noon and we search for a place to eat as we drive through the city down Main Street. Bear sees a sign for a place called the Wake and Bake Cafe and points it out. We look at each other and smile as to say this is the perfect place. I take a left into the parking lot and park in the first available spot.

As we walk up to the place I tell Bear that I hope they have fish tacos and he agrees. We enter and to our delight they do. We both order the Fish Tacos and sit down at a table by one of the front windows. We get our food and it is fantastic, just like home. As we eat we discuss what the plan is and decide to check out Arches for about an hour and then head down to Natural Bridges, bypassing Canyonlands, for the night. Then tomorrow we will check out Monument Valley and then head to the Grand Canyon and camp out there. We are passing up Canyonlands and limiting our time at Arches so we have an excuse to come back and Bear really wants to get to Phoenix.

We head back through town the way we came in, this time north on Highway 191. Just north of town I take a right onto Arches Entrance Road, a twenty-three mile road that meanders through the heart of the park. The road allows us to see many rock structures from my Jeep. On the left, we see the Three

Gossips, a rock formation that looks like three ladies standing and talking. The Organ and the Tower of Babel we pass on our right. As we continue on we see the Great Wall, which is exactly that, a large wall of tan rock on our left.

Then we come across the Balanced Rock to our right, which is exactly that, a large rock that looks like it is balancing on another rock, but it's actually one rock. Nature the artist once again creating masterpieces. We continue to meander down the road, bending left, then right, then left again. Next, we see the Fiery Furnace on our right, a large rock wall, but different from the Great Wall. The rock looks more like individual structures clumped together and not just one solid wall structure. Further down the road we see the Skyline Arch on our right.

We finally reach the end of the road and decided to park and hike a half mile up the Devil's Garden Trail to see a couple more arches. After a short fifteen minute hike north we see the first arch, Landscape Arch, a long, thin arch. All I can think about while I look at it is how one day the wind and rain will destroy it, nature's art eventually fading away, just like us. The second arch, Navajo Arch, is a short, stumpy, thick arch that you can walk through. The next arch is Partition Arch, which looks more like a hole, or actually two holes in the rock, then an arch. The last arch is the Wall Arch, which is my least favorite, but still a nice arch structure. We head back to the Jeep, take the Arches Entrance Road back to Highway 191, and head south back through Moab. We gas up the Jeep, grab some more trail mix and waters, and then continue south towards Natural Bridges National Monument.

A little over an hour later we reach Blanding, Utah. Two miles after that we turn right and head west on Highway 95. Thirty minutes later we take a right on Highway 275 or Natural Bridge Road, the park only five miles away. We stop at the visitor center to check it out and grab a map of the park. We decide to park at the park's campground and just hike around the park from there. The park is pretty compact and it should be an easy hike. We find a spot in the campground and park. We load up our packs with snacks and waters and then head out. There is a road that loops eight miles around all of the natural bridges so we head down it.

We spend the next two hours exploring the park and its bridges, which look exactly like the arches we saw earlier, just lighter in color. This is because they are at a different layer of the Earth' crust. The sun is setting so we start looking for a place to camp for the night. The campground was a little too crowded for our liking and we really don't want to be bothered by other people tonight. We are going to have people all around us in a couple of days when we get to Phoenix and then back in L.A. We find a spot that is off the beaten path a bit so the Rangers won't be able to see us and make us go back to our campsite. We lay our sleeping bags, mats, and pillows out and lie on them. We snack on trail mix and throw back some waters before Bear pulls out a small joint for us to share. He lights it, takes a hit, and passes it to me.

"We should have asked those chicks if they wanted to come with us to Arches and here," Bear says.

"I thought about it."

"So, why didn't you?"

"I don't know, I guess because this is our man trip. Besides we will see them again. I got their numbers, remember?"

"True. I can't believe we didn't try anything with them."

"Yeah, it was weird. I didn't really feel like it. It just seemed perfect just sitting there drinkin' wine, smokin', and talkin'. And as crazy as this sounds, sex or whatever would have ruined it."

"I agree Mad Max, I totally get that. It was perfect how it was. And you're right, we'll see them again."

"Hells yeah we will. We'll go down to San Diego and take those chicks into Tijuana and get into some good old fashion shenanigans, Mexican style."

"Yeah, watch out Mexico, the Zen Lunatics are a comin'," Bear howls and I laugh then tell him to keep it down.

"So where are we staying in Phoenix?" I ask.

"We'll stay with an old college friend of mine, Stacy." Bear went to college at Northern Arizona University in Flagstaff.

"Stacy? An old girlfriend?"

"Nah, just a girl that's a friend."

"Oh, she wasn't interested huh?"

Bear laughs, "Yeah, no, but I'm gonna give it the old college try once again." We both laugh. "We will have a great time man, I'm sure you will hook up with one of her friends,"

Bear says.

"Well duh, that's a given." We laugh again.

The stars are out in force, all of them, billions it looks like. I see a shooting star, which Bear misses, and he asks me if I made a wish. I tell him I did and he asks me what it was. I tell him he knows I can't tell him or it won't come true. He asks if it had something to do with Caroline and I say "maybe." Bear laughs and says "maybe my ass." We laugh again.

"Hey Max, can I ask you a serious question?"

"Of course."

"Do you think we're doing enough with our lives?"

"What do you mean?"

"I don't know, I guess I'm not sure why we're here or at least why I am here. I mean am I here on Earth to drink and smoke and screw and hike and camp and write poetry? Is that my destiny?"

"I think the answer to that question is for each individual to figure out. I can't answer that question for you."

"Well then how would you answer that question for yourself?"

"The why am I here question? I don't know man. I think I'm here to drink and smoke and screw and hike and camp and write." We laugh once again. "But no, seriously I think we're all here to do one thing. And that one thing is to love and to accept love. And I'm not talking about romantic love, I'm talking about unconditional love. I mean the Beatles said it best man, all you need is love. And I don't think they were talking about romantic love because there's more to a romantic relationship then love. I think we're just supposed to love everyone and accept their love in return. I mean can you imagine how different history and society would be if we all loved each other? If we all respected each other? No war, no slavery, no crime, no homelessness, no suicide. Now I know that sounds like a fucking fantasy land but shit man how many times do we fight or argue? How many times do we really fight or argue with any of the people we know? Zero, because we love each other and we respect each other. Anyway, I think hate has taken over our world and we just need to spread more love, that's all."

"Shit Max, you are the reincarnation of Socrates, John Lennon, and Jack Kerouac. A true Zen Lunatic."

"We're all reincarnations of the great people of history. We're all Zen Lunatics. People just don't know it man. They live their lives in fear. They live their lives like sheep, afraid of the wolf, afraid of the unknown. Get in line little sheep, get in line, and do what you're told. Birth, school, work, death. That is life. That is our pathetic existence. But sometimes I do get jealous of the sheep, but then I realize that I'm a sheep, a black sheep for sure, but still a sheep. You are either a sheep or a wolf and as much as I hate being a sheep I would never want to be a wolf. So I become a black sheep and I drink and I smoke and I screw, and I say fuck you sheep and fuck you wolf as I watch them from the top of the mountain. And I laugh and I cry and I wait for death."

"That's fucking brilliant man. Let's meditate on that shit and recharge our batteries. We have a big day tomorrow." I agree and we meditate and we fall asleep under the stars once again and it is beyond words.

We awake again to the sun rising over the landscape to the east. It is still cold out but the sun is warm on our skin as we get out of our sleeping bags and pack up. We head back to the campground and the Jeep and take off back down Natural Bridge Road to Highway 95. A few miles later we take a right and head south on Highway 261 towards Monument Valley. Thirty minutes later we come to a super winding road that leads to the southern Utah valley. As we make our way down the dirt highway, sharply turning left and then right and then left and then right again, we can see the amazing valley and we decide to pull over and soak it in. We climb a large rock feature and we are speechless. The scene in front of us is surreal. We can see the entire southern Utah valley and all of its colors; browns, yellows, oranges, and even some blues. We stand there for several minutes meditating on the natural wonder that is southern Utah.

We climb back down, get in the Jeep, and head back down the winding highway. We reach Highway 163 fifteen minutes later and take a right, heading south. Thirty minutes later we reach Monument Valley Road just north of the Arizona border and take a left. We head east on the road, which crosses over into Arizona. On both sides of the road we see large rock formations that are shooting up out of the ground like they don't belong there. We pull into the parking lot, park, get out and walk towards the visitor center. As we walk up we see more rock formations shooting up out of the ground, these ones are more orange in color and more spectacular. They are monumental and we see why this is called Monument Valley. I have seen these formation before, I think in the film *Close Encounters of the Third Kind*, but I could be wrong. It is surreal. It's like you are looking at a picture or a painting.

We stand there and soak it all in like we did at Zion and Bryce and Arches, and Natural Bridges. This trip has been insane so far and we still have the mother of all National Parks to visit, the Grand Canyon. We head into the visitor center and gift shop where tourists are looking at all of the overpriced souvenirs, fucking capitalism. We use the bathroom and then head back to the Jeep. We head back down the road and enter Utah again before turning left on Highway 163. A minute later we are back in Arizona and three hours from the South Rim of the Grand Canyon.

Twenty-five minutes later we reach Kayenta and I take a right onto Highway 160. An hour later we drive through Tuba City and hit Highway 89 ten minutes after that. I take a left, heading south, and we reach Highway 64 twenty minutes later. I take a right and we head west along the South Rim of the Grand Canyon. An hour later I take a right on Yaki Point Road, which leads us to the South Kaibab Trailhead parking lot. Our plan is to hike down to the Colorado River and sleep on the bank. Then hike back up in the morning and head to

Phoenix. We get out of the Jeep, and just like the past three days, we pack up and head down the trail.

The Colorado River is six miles north and as we head down the trail the views are amazing. It is just like Monument Valley as in it looks fake, like it's a picture or a painting. It is so vast and more beautiful than I had imagined. About a mile and a half in we reach Cedar Ridge and the view here is even more spectacular. We continue on and come across a group on donkeys or mules and we scoot over so they can get by. I make eye contact with one of the animals and he looks at me like please help me and I feel sorry for him. And it reminds me of the main character in the book *Johnny's Got His Gun*. No arms, no legs, no face, no way to communicate except to bang his head against his pillow tapping out kill me in Morse code. At that moment I appreciate my life more than ever.

We pass O'Neill Butte, a large rock formation shooting up towards the clear blue sky. About three miles in we reach Skeleton Point and look over the ridge and see the mighty Colorado River, we are halfway there. Then we reach a place called the Tip Off and we can see the River within reach. The view from here is extraordinary and we stop for a few minutes to soak it in. We observe the different colored layers of the canyon, which give us a look into millions of years of geological history. After a short discussion on the geology of the Grand Canyon, we take off down the trail. We finally reach the Colorado River three hours later at Black Bridge.

The sun is setting as we head east off of the trail to find a spot to camp for the night. We look around to make sure no one sees us but we really don't care. We find a secluded spot on the south bank of the Colorado and set up shop. We lay on our sleeping gear and relax for a while without a word spoken. The sound of the river is soothing and tranquil. This is the essence of Zen lunacy, being off of the beaten path, violating the law, but not hurting anyone, and meditating in the center of the greatest canyon on earth. We smoke a joint and talk a little bit about life and love and beer, which we haven't had since Vegas and are thirsting for. We fall asleep for the fourth night in a row under the stars, but this night is different, this right here has made the trip complete.

I wake to the sounds of people and I prepare for a small army of park rangers that have come to throw us out of here. I sit up and notice a large raft floating down the river with six people inside enjoying the calm rapids. One of them notices me and waves and I wave back. It is time to go. I wake up Bear, we stretch for a bit, pack up, and then head back up to the Jeep. It takes four and a half hours this time and we are starving. We decided to wait until we get to Flagstaff to eat, which is an hour and a half south. We get back on Highway 64, travel south about thirty miles, and merge left onto Highway 180. We take the 180 east and south and we can see Humphrey's Peak in the distance. We pass right by the mountain and enter the city of Flagstaff, Arizona. We stop at a sandwich shop and devour a couple of hot ham and cheese hoagies. We also stop for gas and some energy drinks and then head straight south to Phoenix on Interstate 17.

Two and a half hours later we reach Stacy's apartment, which is in the Phoenix suburb of Chandler. It is still hot here even though it is mid-September, but it feels good and we don't complain. We get out, grab our packs, and head to the front door. Bear knocks four times really hard and yells "police, open up." Stacy yells through the door "show me your badges?" Bear replies in a Mexican accent "badges? We don't need no stinking badges." We laugh and we can hear Stacy laugh behind the door, which immediately opens and we walk in.

CHAPTER SEVEN

Stacy closes the door and tells us to follow her to the guest bedroom that we will be sharing over the next three days. We throw our packs at the foot of the bed and I jump on it and tell Stacy that this will work and that there is plenty of room for Bear and I to spoon each other to sleep. She laughs as I hop off of the bed. I realize that I have not introduced myself, or that Bear has not introduced me, so I do so. Bear apologizes and he is forgiven immediately.

We ask if we can shower and do a load of laundry and she says "of course." She tells us to get a move on because she has some friends coming over soon. I inquire if they are of the female persuasion and she assures me that they are and that a couple of them are single. I smile and then we grab our packs and follow her to the laundry room. While Bear showers I start a load of laundry. Stacy yells from the kitchen if I want a beer and I yell back that I do. I walk into the kitchen and she hands me a bottle of Sierra Nevada Pale Ale, a great beer, which is brewed in Chico.

Bear enters the kitchen ten minutes later in only a towel. "I smell beer," he says. Stacy opens the fridge, grabs a beer, opens it, and hands it to Bear. As he grabs for it he lets go of his towel and it falls to the floor. Bear is frozen, standing there naked, with his right arm straight out holding a cold beer. He takes a drink of his beer before grabbing his towel and Stacy and I laugh. He walks out of the kitchen, still bare-assed. We continue to laugh. I finish my beer and then head back to the laundry room and put the clothes from the washer into the dryer and start it.

I head to the guest bathroom and take a shower. The water feels amazing, there is nothing better than a hot shower after you have been out in nature for four days. I finish up my shower and head back to the kitchen to grab another beer, in only a towel. I make sure the towel does not fall to the floor. Bear and Stacy are in the living room and I head there. I sit on the couch next to Bear, both of us are only in towels, because all of our clothes are in the dryer. The three of us are enjoying our beers and relaxing when we hear a knock at the door.

Three knocks and then the door opens, before we can even react, and it is three of Stacy's girlfriends. They freeze as soon as they walk in, the scene, unexpected. Stacy is sitting in her living room with two guys that they don't know, wearing only towels. Bear breaks the awkwardness by crossing his legs, exposing himself to the ladies, and in the process making it even more awkward. The ladies get that look on their face, you know, the look a chick gets on her face when she sees something gross.

"Hey ladies," Stacy says, breaking the silence. The ladies all say hey.

"This is my old friend from college, Bear, and his friend Max." Bear and I raise our beers and say hi and they say hi back. They are not sure what to do so they head to the kitchen to put away the drinks that they had brought with them. Stacy smiles at us and we smile back as she heads to the kitchen to explain to her friends what they just saw. Bear and I look at each other and laugh.

We finish our beers and like clockwork the dryer buzzes. We head to the laundry room, pull our clothes out of the dryer, and head to the guest bedroom. We get dressed, pack up the rest of our clothes, and head to the kitchen for some beers. The ladies are in Stacy's bedroom and bathroom at the moment, so we decide to check out the back porch. It is a second story apartment so we can see most of the complex. I notice a swimming pool about fifty feet to the right of us and I tell Bear that we will be in it by the end of the night. He agrees. The ladies are finally finished doing whatever it is women do in the bathroom when they are already ready and enter the kitchen. We turn and look into the kitchen through the patio doors.

"So, which one do you like?" I ask.

"I don't know, are they all single?"

"I don't see any wedding rings." I say after looking at their left hands.

"Doesn't mean they don't have a boyfriend."

"Boyfriend, Shmoyfriend," We laugh.

"Okay, let's assume they are all single, which one are you feelin'?" I ask.

"I like the look of that brunette with the blue top on."

"Okay, not my favorite, so she's yours. I think I am feeling the blond."

"Wow, what a surprise." I look at Bear and smile real big.

"Alright, let's go in and get this party started."

We walk into the kitchen and all the ladies look at us and we smile. They are all drinking some sort of yellowish green cocktail, which I assume is a margarita.

"Hello boys. Margarita?" Stacy asks lifting her drink. We lift our beers as to say no we're good.

"So guys, this is Karen." She points to the brunette in the green top right next to her. "That is Rebecca, but we just call her Becca" She points to the brunette with the blue top next to Karen. "And that is Julie." She points to the blonde standing next to Becca. We say hello and introduce ourselves again.

"Tequila shots?" I suggest to the group, while I am looking at Julie.

"You read my mind," Julie says. The rest of the ladies agree.

Stacy goes to a cabinet and pulls out six shot glasses. Karen grabs a couple limes from the fridge and Becca grabs the salt shaker. Stacy grabs the tequila and pours it into the shot glasses, while Karen cuts up the limes. Stacy passes out the shots and Karen passes out the limes. Julie licks her hand and sprinkles a little salt on it, she passes it around and we all do the same. I lift my shot glass and everyone else follows.

"Here's to a safe and sober night," I exclaim, smiling. Everyone laughs, then we lick the salt, take the shot, and suck on the lime.

"One more?" Julie asks.

"Giddy up," I say. And right on cue Stacy pours another round while Karen gets more limes ready.

We call a van cab and jump in when it arrives. We head to a place called Dos Gringos, which is a typical Mexican bar party place, with Corona and tequila shots on special, which is fire with us. We find a large circular table and the ladies wait there while Bear and I go get drinks at the bar. We return with six Coronas, each with a lime in its mouth. As we drink our first round, I start up a conversation with Julie and we chat about the usual, where we are from, our jobs, etc. Bear is talking to Becca. Stacy and Karen are talking and checking out the male scenery.

We are ready for round two so Bear and I go back up to the bar and return with six more Coronas, but this time they are a little different. These are loaded Coronas, which means the bartender poured tequila into the Corona bottle. I tell everyone that they have to put their thumb on the top of the bottle and turn it upside-down to mix the tequila into the beer, which everyone does. Then I tell them to take a drink before they put the lime in or the bottle will overflow and make a mess, which everyone does. Then we cram our limes into our bottles and continue to drink.

The rest of the night was filled with more drinking, of course, and chatting and even some dancing. Julie and I are hitting it off, Bear and Becca seem to be into each other, and Stacy and Karen have been talking to two guys for an hour or so. At last call we decided to leave. Julie, Becca, Bear, and I jump into a cab, while Stacy and Karen get a ride with the two guys they were talking to. I tell the cab driver to follow them just in case they try to kidnap our friends.

Both vehicles arrive at Stacy's apartment complex at the same time. I pay the driver, we get out, and head to Stacy's apartment. As we walk up the stairs, Stacy is unlocking the door, Karen and the two guys are with her. We all enter and take seats in the living room, except for Bear, who runs to the spare room to grab something. Several seconds later I see Bear trying to secretly get my attention from the hallway. I notice him, he shows me a joint, and through some really crude sign language he tells me to grab the girls and meet him on the porch. I nod acknowledging that I understand. I tell Julie that if she and Becca want to smoke a joint, Bear and I will be out on the back porch. She says okay and I leave, walking through the kitchen and joining Bear on the porch.

"Where are the girls?" Bear asks.

I look through the patio doors and see them coming. "They're comin' man, relax." I open the door and the two ladies walk through and join us on the porch. Bear lights the joint and takes a hit.

"So have you ladies smoked before?" I ask.

Julie answers, "I have but it's been awhile."

"I did last night," Becca adds, smiling.

Bear passes the joint to Becca and says, "Well here ya go." She takes it, takes a hit, and passes it to Julie, who takes a hit, and passes it to me. I take a hit and pass it back to Bear.

I notice the pool again and suggest that the four of us should take a dip. Becca does not like the idea, but Julie is down, so after a couple more hits on the joint we go back inside, grab a couple of towels and sneak out of the apartment. When we get to the pool gate we notice that it is locked and that we need a key to get in. Julie runs back up and gets the key from Stacy while I wait.

She returns and we enter the pool area. There is no one there but us; perfect. We throw our towels on the side of the pool, strip down to our underwear, and hop into the shallow end. The water is warm thanks to the Phoenix sun. We stand there looking at each other for several seconds before I make my way over to her. I slowly put my right hand on her hip to see where I stand and she puts her arms around my neck. I place my left hand on her other hip and kiss her. She pulls me in tighter as we kiss.

We kiss for a couple more minutes, then Julie lets go of me, puts her arms behind her back, and takes her bra off. Her breasts are a full B-cup and still perky. She then reaches down and removes her panties and I follow by removing my boxers. We kiss again. A minute or so later she reaches down and grabs my family jewels. I repay the favor and start touching her nether region. At that moment we hear Becca yelling from the apartment porch.

"Julie!"

We ignore her.

"Julie!" Louder this time.

"What the fuck?" I say, pissed at the terrible timing.

Again she yells, "Julie, come here."

Julie yells back, "What?"

"I need you to come up here right now," Becca yells back.

"It must be important. Let me see what she wants real quick."

"Okay." I am not happy at all.

Julie gets out, dries off, puts her clothes back on, and heads back to the apartment. Five minutes pass and I start to get pissed so I get out, dry off, put my clothes back on, and head back upstairs. When I open the door everyone but Becca and Julie are in the living room laughing.

"What's up Mad Max?" Bear says with a smile. Everyone laughs louder.

"Where's Julie? What the fuck happened?"

"Oh they're in Stacy's room talking," Bear answers.

"Talking about what? What the hell was so important?"

"You should go see man."

I agree and head to Stacy's room. When I get there I knock on the door. Becca opens the door and gives me the dirtiest look I have ever seen.

"What the hell do you want?" she barks.

"What is going on? Did I do something?" I can hear Julie crying.

"Did you do something? Are you serious?" she barks back even louder and angrier.

"I don't know what's happening here, can you just tell me?" I say, confused.

"Um, you're married, that is what's happening here."

"Married? I'm not fucking married. Who the hell told you that?"

"Um, Bear did."

"Well he's a fucking liar and a dead man. I will be back after I kick his ass. Can you tell her that this is all a twisted joke and that I am not married? Hell I don't even have a girlfriend."

"So you're not married?"

"No."

Her attitude changes from being mad at me to being furious with Bear. "No, you talk to Julie, I will take care of Bear." Becca rushes by me and heads to the living room, I assume to give Bear the beating of a lifetime.

I enter the bedroom and Julie is on the bed wiping tears from her eyes and face.

"I'm not married. That was just a horrible joke."

I did not expect what happened next to occur. Julie starts laughing and I am standing there confused, not knowing what to think or what to do. Then there is an arm around me and I turn my head and see Bear, Becca next to him, and Stacy behind them.

"Why is it that you always make women laugh Mad Max?" Bear says.

"What the fuck is going on? I'm so confused."

"A prank within a prank my friend."

"What?"

Bear starts laughing. "I told Becca that you were married so she yelled at Julie to come up here so she could tell her. But before Julie got here I told Becca that I was kidding and that I just wanted to fuck with you. Then when Julie got up here I told her that I wanted to fuck with you some more so we continued the married story."

They are all laughing now. "We got you good Mad Max, we got you good man."

I can't be mad, it was a good one, and I start laughing along with them. I walk over to Julie and lie down on the bed next to her. I tell her that was messed up and then kiss her. Bear and Becca leave.

Stacy pops her head in and says "don't worry about the

sheets, I will wash them tomorrow."

She turns off the light and closes the door. We continue to kiss and end up fucking like wild animals for about thirty minutes. When we finish we head to the kitchen for some more liquid refreshment. We drink a couple more beers and take a couple more tequila shots. It is almost four in the morning and we are hammered so we decide to hit the sack. Stacy tells us to just take her room since we already destroyed it. We get to the room and pass out within seconds of hitting the pillows. About an hour later I wake up, because I really have to use the bathroom. When I get back to the room I can't believe what I see, Julie is squatting on the floor next to the bed pissing on the carpet. I stand there in shock. It is the longest piss ever and when she finishes she just falls over and passes out in the puddle of her own urine. I am too exhausted to deal with this so I just climb back in bed and pass out again.

When I wake up, Julie is gone, but the smell of her piss still lingers in the air. Bear storms in and is hit in the nose with the smell.

"Dude, did you piss the bed?"

I start laughing, "No." I laugh louder. "Julie pissed the floor." I continue to laugh, even louder now.

"What?"

"I went to the bathroom, came back, and she was pissing on the carpet. She passed out right on it and I just got back in bed and passed out." I am laughing so hard it hurts now.

"No fucking way." Bear starts laughing with me.

I get up and we head to the kitchen where Stacy is cleaning up.

"Hey, when you are done with that, we have something else that needs to be cleaned up," Bear says. We chuckle and Stacy is confused.

"Your friend Julie pissed on the carpet in your bedroom," I explain.

Stacy's mouth opened wide in disbelief, "are you shitting me? You're shitting me right?"

I shake my head, "nope, totally serious."

"Un-fucking-believable," she says, shaking her head. "Fuck that, I'm gonna call that bitch and she is gonna get her blond ass back over here and clean that shit up."

"You mean clean that piss up?" Bear says, smiling. I laugh but stop after seeing the look on Stacy's face.

I change the subject. "So are there any mountains we can climb here in the desert?"

"Of course there are. Just give me a few minutes to get ready, I will make us some pancakes, and then we can head out," Bear says.

"Stacy cuts in, still pissed about the pee, "Um, you're not making pancakes in this fucking kitchen, I just cleaned it; take your asses to IHOP."

We laugh, Stacy gives us an, I'm going to kill you look, and we immediately stop laughing. We go to the guest bedroom and change into shorts and hiking shoes. We head out and stop at an IHOP on the way for some pancakes. We take a seat in a booth by the front entrance.

"So where or what are we hiking?" I ask.

"The backside of South Mountain. It's a short one, about five miles round trip with a nice elevation change. There is a cool rock gazebo about halfway up and the view at the top of the trail is insane. You can see the entire Phoenix Valley, well most of it anyway."

"Sounds good."

We each order a short stack of pancakes coffee, and one side order of bacon, to share. We eat, pay, and then head west through Ahwatukee, a small neighborhood west of Chandler on the southern base of South Mountain. We make our way to the trailhead parking lot, get out, and start up the trail. The first half mile is wide and paved and there are quite a few people on it. Bear tells me not to worry, that the crowds will thin out as we make our way up. The pavement ends and turns to dirt and rock as we head up the backside of the mountain. I say mountain loosely because it is not really a mountain, but it's not a hill either, I guess it's kind of in between, maybe a small mountain. A half mile later we reach a paved road. Bear tells me that the road leads to the top of South Mountain and that the entrance is on the north side. He says this is not the end of our hike as we walk down the road a hundred yards and jump back on the trail.

A half mile later we reach the rock gazebo that Bear told me about earlier. It is a little smaller than other, wooden gazebos that I have seen, mainly in parks and people s backyards. There isn't a roof on it, but it does have a barbeque, seating, and a table in it, all made of stone of course. We decide to climb it to get a better view of the south valley and just because we want to climb it. After soaking in the view, Bear tells me that the better view is awaiting us just three quarters of a mile up the trail, so we get down off the stone gazebo, and continue on the dirt and rock trail. Bear was right, the people have thinned out up here, I haven't seen anyone in several minutes, but I can still hear people below us.

We reach the end of our hike, but apparently not the trail, because it looks like it continues on for miles and miles. The view as we walk up is spectacular, just like Bear had described. You can see most of the valley, including downtown Phoenix, Sun Devil Stadium along with the rest of Arizona State University and all of the west valley, which still has quite a bit of farmland left. I look farther north, and it is so clear out, I swear I can see Humphrey's peak in Flagstaff from here.

I always love looking down on cities from high above, they are so quiet and peaceful. Like when I fly into L.A or any city for that matter. You look out that small window and you know that it is chaos down there, people yelling at each other, cops chasing drug dealers, car's honking during rush hour. But from high above, it's what you want it to be, or more importantly what you wish it was like, and really, what you hoped one day it would be. From up here Phoenix looked like a picture or a painting, nothing moving, just there, peaceful, showing us what it could be.

Our standing meditation is interrupted by a couple that has made their way up to where we are so we head back down, running this time, I almost die twice and almost twist my ankle four times, but we both make it to the Jeep uninjured and alive, in record time. We head back to Stacy's, but stop on the way to buy more beers. Our plan is to be poolside, drinking beers by the top of the hour. When we get back to Stacy's, she and Karen are on the back porch smoking, so we join them.

"How was the hike?" Stacy asks.

"It was good," Bear answers.

"The view up there was amazing," I add.

"Yeah, I have done that hike many times and the view is spectacular," adds Karen.

"So what's the plan today?" Bear asks.

"I don't know, what do you want to do?" Stacy replies.

"Get drunk and high, maybe get laid, you know, the usual," Bear says.

We all laugh. "That is your usual, except for the getting laid part." I say. We all laugh again, a little louder this time.

"Ha, Ha, real funny. I will bet you that I get laid tonight."

"What's the bet?" I ask.

"The bar tab."

"Okay, but you have to pay the tab and if you do score I will reimburse you. Deal?"

"Deal."

"Oh, and it has to be a real chick, no dolls, no animals, no dudes, and definitely no couches."

"Couches?" Karen says, confused.

I start laughing, "Tell them the couch story."

"No way," Bear says, looking at me like he can't believe I brought that up.

"Come on, it was like fifteen years ago, just tell them," I am smiling ear to ear.

"Alright, fuck it. It is a pretty funny story."

"Funny? It's fuckin' hilarious," I add.

Well I was about thirteen and was home alone one day after school. I was going through puberty and I was getting boners, every day, several times a day. I would even get boners in class looking at all the girls and I would have to think about something else to get my boner down before the bell rang. Anyway, I was home alone this one time and I was tired of just jerking off so I decided to experiment. Now our couch was really soft and felt good when you laid on it so I thought I would give it a shot."

Stacy and Karen have confused looks on their faces.

"To make a short story shorter, I fucked the couch."

They could not believe what he had just said and were silent for a few seconds before they busted out laughing.

"You fucked your couch?" Stacy asked just to make sure she heard right.

"Yep, I fucked my couch."

I starting laughing with the girls. "Who fucks a couch?"

Karen says, still laughing.

"Apparently I do." Bear says, embarrassed as hell.

"Dude, I'm sure plenty of thirteen year olds have screwed their couches. There are probably some screwing their couches right now," I say.

"Did you screw your couch?" Stacy asks me.

"Hell no, I'm not a weirdo," I answer as I look at Bear. The three of us are laughing harder now.

"Dick," Bear says, still embarrassed and wishing he had not told the story.

"Oh quit your pouting. I'm just messin' with you man. You know I love you."

We tell the girls that we are going to hit the pool and ask them if they want to join us. They do, so I throw some beers in a cooler, Karen grabs some towels, and Stacy grabs her radio. The four of us head down to the pool, drink some beers, soak in some rays, and swim a little, while listen to some music. We spend an hour poolside and then head back up to the Apartment and take a nap, the sun and beers have worn us out. We wake up and chill for a bit before getting ready for the night ahead. Bear tells me that we are going to go see an old friend of his in Tempe tonight and that we will hit up the bars down there. His place is in walking distance to the bars so we will just head out from there and then crash at his place. He invites Stacy and Karen, but they say they are just going to stay in for the night.

We shower, get dressed, and leave. We arrive at his buddy's

place twenty minutes later. Bear knocks on the front door and someone inside yells "come on in," which we do. There is a guy and a girl sitting on the couch. I wonder, at that moment, if Bear is getting all hot and bothered seeing the couch and I chuckle. Bear looks at me like, what are you laughing at?

"Barry Manilow, what the fuck man?" the guys says. He stands up and gives Bear a hug, a literal and figurative Bear hug.

"What's going on man?" Bear asks.

"Just chillin' man, just chillin'. Hey, this is my girlfriend Tammy." He point to the girl on the couch.

Bear leans over and shakes her hand. "This is my buddy Max." He shoots his thumb towards me and I shake his hand and he tells me his name is Nate. I tell him that it is good to meet him and then I wave hello to Tammy. We take a seat and Bear catches up with Nate for about a half hour while Tammy and I listen in.

"So what's the plan? What kind of trouble you guys wanna get into tonight?" Nate asks.

"Well, whatever gives me the best chance to get laid. I have a bet to win," Bear answers.

"What's the bet?" Nate asks.

I chime in, "If he doesn't get laid he pays the bar tab."

"For all of us?"

"Yeah, the bet was the entire tab," I say.

"Well shit, we have to take him to the hardest place to get laid then."

"Where is that?" asks Tammy.

Nate thinks for a few seconds. "The strip club?"

"I don't think so," Tammy says.

"Yeah fuck that, I don't have the money to pay that tab." Bear chimes in.

"I'm just messin' around. How about Fat Tuesday's on Mill Avenue? You might have a shot at some poon there."

"Poon? Real classy Nate," Tammy says as she gives him the why are you such a child look.

"I think we should take him to Scottsdale. Maybe Martini Ranch?" Tammy suggests.

"Are you driving?" Nate asks.

"Yeah, I'll drive, I drank enough last night."

"Sweet, then it's settled. Martini Ranch it is. We'll take the Excursion, just in case you guys end up bringing some chicks back."

"Sounds good," Bear says and I agree.

We head out just as the clock strikes ten. Fifteen minutes later we park and walk up to the bar. After we show our ID's, we enter. It is a decent crowd for a Sunday night and the male to female ratio seems even. Bear assess the situation immediately. We grab a table and Nate heads to the bar to order three beers and a water. He returns with the drinks and asks Bear if he see his first victim yet. Bear says he is still checking out the scenery and will get back to me. We spend the next two hours drinking and chatting. Tammy gets Nate on the dance floor a couple of times while we continue to look for two chicks to hit on. We finally see two that might be worthy of our company and we discuss our plan of attack. I tell him that I have the perfect plan and I quickly get up and walk towards the girls, leaving Bear at the table without telling him my plan.

I approach them and say, "excuse me ladies." They turn and look at me. "If you two are single and interested I would love to buy you both a drink." They check me out.

"Sure," the black-haired chick says.

"Cool, what are you drinkin'?"

"Apple martinis," the redhead says. I think, of course you are.

"Okay, two apple martinis. I will be right back." As I make my way to the bar I look at Bear and give him the thumbs up and he nods his head and smiles. I grab the drinks, head back over to the girls, and set their drinks on the table.

"So I'm Max. What are your names?"

"I'm Jill," the redhead says.

"I'm Corrie," the dark-haired chick says.

"Nice to meet both of you. So here's the deal, you see that guy over there?" I point to Bear and they acknowledge that they do. "Well that is my friend Barry and he told me this morning that he's gay." They look back at me like, what did you just say? "Yeah, I know, crazy huh? Well to make a long story short I asked him how he knew and blah, blah, blah, I come to find out that he has never been with a woman. So I told him that he should probably sleep with a chick before he makes such a rash lifestyle decision." They look back at him and then back at me. "Now, I'm usually not this forward, but you are smoking hot, I mean it, a fucking goddess. And I would love to hang out with you tonight," I say to Jill, the redhead. "And don't get me wrong, you're hot too, I just have a thing for redheads." Which is a lie, but whatever. "So, I'm gonna head back over to my friends, you two talk about it, and if you are down, come on over." I walk away before they can say anything.

When I get back to the table Tammy and Nate are back from dancing. "So, what's up with that Mad Max?" Nate asks.

"I'm not sure. I threw the line out. We shall see if they bite."

"What did you say?" Bear asks.

"Well, here's the deal. They think you're gay." Tammy and Nate start laughing.

"What?"

"Yeah, but just listen. I told them that you told me that you had never been with a woman before. So, if they do come over then that means the dark-haired chick, Corrie wants to bang the gay out of you." Tammy and Nate laugh even louder.

"Why the dark-haired chick and not the redhead?" Bear asks.

"Well because I told the redhead, Jill, that I basically wanted to bang her. Now, they are talking right now and one of two things is gonna happen. One, they decide that we are insane and probably bullshitting them and they stay put. Or two, they decide that we are insane and probably bullshitting them, but they still want to fuck us and they come over."

"No way they come over here," Tammy says.

"Not a chance," adds Nate.

At that moment, Bear's eyes look passed me and get wide. "I think they're coming." Tammy and Nate look and then they look at me and I smile.

"Un-fucking-believable," Nate says.

The girls walk up and stand in between Bear and I. I introduced everyone and we spend the next hour drinking and chatting and dancing. We shut the bar down and head outside. We all decide that we are starving and need some late night eats. So we head to the Denny's down the street. We are hammered, except for Tammy since she is our designated driver. Corrie and Jill took a cab to the bar so they just rode with us. We sit at the first empty table we see and a white guy with dreadlocks walks up to us.

"Can I get you guys some drinks?"

"Coffees and waters all around," I yell.

"But I don't want coffee," Jill says to me.

"Don' worry, I'll drink it," I say.

We peruse the menus while Mr. Dreadlocks gets our drinks. He returns with the waters, sets them down, and leaves to get the coffees.

Just as he leaves I say "what is up with those dreadlocks?" not to him to the group, but loud enough for him to hear me.

"Dude, he heard you," Bear says.

"I don't care," I say, drunk as fuck.

He returns with the coffees and takes our order. I am the last one to order.

"And what can I get for you?"

With a straight face I say, "Um, I'll have the mothafuckin' Super Bird."

The entire table starts laughing and Mr. Dreadlocks rolls his eyes and is probably thinking that he doesn't get paid enough to deal with this shit. Our food comes, we eat, we laugh, and we almost get kicked out. We finish eating, pay, leave a nice big tip, and then we head back to Nate's place. Corrie and Jill are sitting in the very back of the Excursion. Bear and I are in the middle row. Nate is in the front passenger seat and Tammy is driving.

As we make our way back to Nate's, Corrie and Jill start making out. All of us are staring, even Tammy, but then she realizes what she is doing and elbows Nate, who stops looking. We get to Nate's and head inside. Nate and Tammy call it a night and head off to bed. We sit in the living room, Bear and I on the couch, Corrie and Tammy on the loveseat. They waste no time and begin to make out with each other again. Corrie pushes Jill down and lays on top of her. We are like deer in headlights, staring, we can't stop looking; it is mesmerizing. After about ten minutes they stop.

Corrie looks at Bear, "So, you've never slept with a woman?" At this question all I can think of is shit, I lost the bet.

"Nope," he answers.

"Well, come on over here and give it a try." Bear and Jill switch places. We banged them, right there in the living room. And when we were done, we switched places, and banged the other one. When we woke up, they were still there, so we quietly snuck out and headed back over to Stacy's. Nate called Bear an hour later, laughing and cursing at him for leaving two naked chicks in his living room. He said Tammy woke up and saw them, woke them up, and took them home. She said it was the most awkward situation she has ever been in. Bear apologized and Nate said not to worry about it, it was too insane to be mad over.

At Stacy's, we went back to sleep for a few hours. We woke up, said our goodbyes, and then went to get some In N' Out Burger's before we headed home to L.A. The drive home was quick, about five hours. I spent a good hour of the trip passing gas in silence waiting for Bear to smell it. And then watching him try to put the window down, which he couldn't because I had the window lock on. That shit was too funny, especially when he threatened to open the door and jump out if I did not stop. We did stop once for gas, in Blythe, California, and made it home just as the sun set over the beautiful Pacific Ocean. It was the perfect ending to the perfect Zen Lunatic road trip.

CHAPTER EIGHT

Three months after our road trip through Nevada, Utah, and Arizona I get a call from Rob saying that he is coming down to L.A the day after Christmas, which is just a week away. He asks if he can crash at our place until after the New Year and I tell him of course he can. Rob arrives the evening of December 26th and I set him up in my room with an inflatable mattress, complete with sheets, a blanket and a pillow. Drew is at work and Bear is out somewhere unknown to me, so Rob and I head out to grab some beers at a local market. Rob is starving so we stop at my favorite Mexican place, Tito's Tacos.

The place is packed, like it is every hour of every day, but we order within five minutes. There are a dozen workers in this place, all Mexicans, and all running around taking orders and filling them. When it is our turn I order a meat and cheese burrito, a taco with cheese, and a diet Coke, the usual and Rob orders the same. We sit outside on one of the picnic style benches and wait for our food. The man who took our order and grabbed our food, calls out the order and I go up to window, pay for it, grab it, and head back to our table. We eat and it tastes just as good as it does every time, just as good as it did when I was a kid. Rob is blown away by how good it tastes.

"You weren't kidding Mad Max, this is insanely good."

"I told you man, this is why I won't leave L.A, at least for a long period of time."

"So, when was the last time you talked to Caroline?" Rob asks.

"I don't know, like three or four months ago, ever since she told me about the guy from school."

"Hmm."

"What?"

"A couple of weeks ago she asked me if I had your number and I said of course I did. Then she asked if she could have it and I said sure and I gave it to her. She didn't call you?"

"Nope."

"Hmm, that's strange, why would she ask me for it if she wasn't gonna call you?"

"I don't know, maybe she lost my number and just wanted

it for whatever reason. Is she still with that guy?"

"I assume they're still together, he was over at our place last week, after she asked for your number."

"Hmm, that is a little strange."

"Maybe she is thinking of ending things with him?"

"I guess that's possible, but why wouldn't she wait to ask you for my number after they split up? And how did she lose my number in the first place? Did she delete it from her phone?"

"I don't know. Maybe she wanted me to tell you that she asked for your number?"

"So I would call her and see what's up?"

"Maybe."

"Shit, I don't know, chicks are too damn hard to figure out sometimes."

"Ain't that the truth?"

"Should I call her?"

"I wouldn't. She knows that I'm here with you and might be expecting you to call since she knows that I probably told you about her asking for your number."

"Yeah. I still don't think I handled that last phone conversation the right way."

"How so?"

"I fucking lied to her man. I told her I was happy for her and wished her luck and all that shit. I should have just told her the truth."

"And what's the truth?"

"That ever since I met her I can't stop thinking about her. And that I think I'm in love with her."

"No shit? You're really in love with her?"

"Yeah, I mean when you called me and told me about her possibly being with a guy I instantly got sick to my stomach. Then when I called her and she confirmed it, my heart hurt, like I literally thought I was having a massive heart attack. I have spent the past three months trying to forget about her and the only way I can do that is to be with other chicks. And sometimes that doesn't even work."

"Maybe you should call her and tell her how you feel?"

"I don't want to break them up, as stupid as that might sound. But if they ever do break up, I might give it another try."

"Dude, if you love her as much as it sounds like you do, you need to tell her man. Forget that she has a boyfriend, she needs to know how you feel. She thinks you are cool with it, she has no idea how you feel. What if she marries this guy?"

"Maybe you're right. Let me think about it for a few days. Now eat up, we have some drinking to do."

We finish our food and head back to the pad. Drew is there chillin' in the living room drinking a beer and watching some World War II battle footage on the History Channel.

"Hey Rob, what's up man?"

"Nada, Drew, what's up with you?"

"Same shit, different day."

Rob sits down on the loveseat, while I take the beers to the kitchen. I throw the thirty pack in the fridge and grab two before closing the fridge door. I walk back into the living room and hand Rob one of the beers. I take a seat next to Drew, open my beer, take a swig, and put my arm around him.

"So whatcha watchin' Drew blew?"

Before he can answer, the front door flies open and Bear comes storming in, closing the door behind him like he was being chased by a mad wild Sasquatch. He looks at us, eyes wide, his back to the door, barricading it with his body.

"Dude, what are you doing?" I ask.

He puts his right index finger to this lips telling us to be quiet. At that moment there is a sudden knock on the door. Bear's finger still pressed to his lips reminding us not to say anything.

"Bear, I know you're in there, I saw you run inside," a female voice screams from the other side.

I start laughing, but not loud, and Bear looks at me, slapping his lips with his finger trying to get me to stop.

"Bear, don't be like this, I just want to talk," the voice says.

I look at Rob, who looks confused. Drew is silent laughing like me. I can't take it anymore, I have to say something.

In a female Chinese accent I say, "No Bears here, now go away." Drew is in tears. Bear is shaking his head violently.

The voice behind the door says, "You guys are stupid."

In the same voice I add, "No Bears here, go to zoo, go to forest." Drew and I and even Bear cannot control ourselves any longer and we all start bust out laughing and I am sure she hears us as she walked back down the street. Rob is still clueless so I explain.

"That was Teresa." who is not unlike a mad wild Sasquatch.

"Who's Teresa?"

"Teresa is Bear's future wife," I say as I smile at Bear.

"Real funny man."

"No seriously, Teresa is this crazy bitch that Bear slept with a couple of months ago. He met her at our friends Halloween party. So picture this, the three of us hanging out drinking beers all dressed up in our costumes and then this chick walks in wearing a dick costume."

"A dick costume?"

"Yeah, a life sized dick costume. It's like one of those ones you fill with air or something. You are literally inside a huge dick. I mean the balls are at your feet and your face is poking out right below the dickhead. The funny part is that it's a guy's costume, why the hell would a chick dress up as a huge dick?"

"Maybe she's a lesbian and she is making some sort of statement?" Rob says.

"Right? That's what we came up with, but Bear decides that he is going to talk to her because he needs to know what is up with the costume. So he goes over and talks to her while Drew and I wait. He returns like a half hour later and we ask him what is up. He starts laughing and tells us that she told him that the party was a last minute thing so she went to a costume shop just an hour ago. She asked the guy behind the

counter for the Venus costume and the guy grabbed it, she paid
for it, and then she ran home to put it on and come to the party.
When she got home she opened the package and it was not a
Venus costume, it was a penis costume. She's Mexican and the
guy at the costume shop heard penis, not Venus."

We all start laughing.

I continue, "So Bear doesn't talk to her until later that night
and by this time we are all hammered. Drew and I have given
up on trying to find chicks to bang, so we go out back, jump in
the hot tub and smoke some weed. About an hour later we are
chillin' on the back porch with the guy who threw the party, by
this time most of the guest have gone home. We hear the patio
door open and Bear is standing there, naked, with blood all
over his crotchal region. It was everywhere, on his dick, his
balls, his stomach, his thighs, fucking everywhere. We are all
in shock and nothing is said for like five seconds, until I say
"dude, did you just murder that chick with your dick?" and he
says "I don't know."

Rob's eyes are wide, his mouth wider.

I continue, "so we don't know what to think about his
answer so the three of us run inside and find her on our
buddy's bed, not moving. She is lying there, blood all over the
white sheets, dude it looked like a fucking massacre, so I go
over to see if she's alive, which she is, just drunk as fuck. We
leave the room in haste and tell Bear to go take a shower and
clean that nastiness off, which he does. Ever since that night
that chick, who just happens to live like five houses down, has

been trying to get with Bear again and he ain't havin' it."

"No I am not. I still can't get that *CSI* scene out of my head bro." We all laugh as Bear heads to the kitchen to grab a beer.

"You guys need a refill?"

"Yes sir, Mr. Bloodycrotch," Drew yells.

"Screw you dickface. You can get your own."

We are sitting in the living room drinking beers and watching the history of the Panama Canal on the History Channel, when I get a call from a buddy of ours. He says that he has a new girlfriend and that he wants to impress her. I tell him I am listening. He wants to know if he can bring her by and if we could have a poetry reading and maybe a little guitar jam. I tell him that I need to confer with my roommates and that he should call me back in five minutes. He says okay and we hang up.

"Who was that?" asks Bear.

"Jeff."

"What does that douche want?" ask Drew.

"He wants to impress his new chick with some mad poetry and guitar music. What do you think?"

"I'm down for a reading and some tunes man," Bear says.

"Yeah, I'm cool with that," Rob replies.

I look at Drew, who hates Jeff with a passion because he ate out his older sister when we were in high school and Drew never got over it. "Drew? Yes? Cool?"

"Fucking I guess, but I have a bet I want to make."

"Lay it on us man," I say.

"I bet I can steal Jeff's new girl buy the end of the night. If I do, I don't have to clean a goddamn thing in this house for a month. If I don't, then I will clean the house."

"I'll take that bet," Bear jumps in.

I think about it for a few seconds and decide that I want to change the bet. "I like the, if you do, but if you don't I want you to drive me wherever I need to go for a month."

"I'm good with that," Drew agrees.

"Okay, then I'm in."

Jeff calls back and I tell him the fiesta is on, but he has to bring three boxes of red wine and tell his girl to bring a couple friends. He agrees, I tell him to be here at ten, and I hang up. I look at Rob and Bear.

"Alright fuckers, game on. Drew! Beers! Stat!" I yell.

Drew gets up and grabs us some beers.

Like clockwork Jeff knocks on the door at ten. We are all still posted up in the living room.

"Come on in," Bear yells.

Jeff opens the door and walks in, three Asian chicks each holding a box of wine shuffle in after him. Rob and I stand up and offer the ladies the couch. They set the wine on the coffee table and take a seat. Jeff sits on the floor, we assume, in front of his new girl, while Rob and I go grab some red plastic cups for the wine.

"Hmm, Asians," I say.

"I've never done an Asian chick before," Rob says.

"Me either."

We head back into the living room and I hand each person a red plastic cup. We start to fill up our cups one at a time. Jeff introduces us to the ladies and we discover that they might be Asian but they are from the Valley and they talk like they are from the Valley and they have Valley names. They are not real Asians.

Bear starts off the poetry reading with a new poem about our trip through the National Parks in Utah and Arizona. He captures the essence of what we experienced, the colors, the textures, the immense landscape, it is a beautiful poem. I go next and read an, oldie but goodie, about love and how it is unattainable in the capacity that we need it to be. Drew reads a poem about the beach, which seems to be a common topic in his poetry. The poem discusses the beach as an analogy for life and loss. I have heard this one many times before and I really like it. He reads it more passionately than I have ever seen him read a poem, obviously trying to impress Jeff's girlfriend.

We drink more wine and read more poetry over the next hour. Then I suggest to Jeff that he grab Bear's guitar and play a few songs for us. He agrees and in no time we are jamming out to Jeff playing songs by the Beatles, the Eagles, and Pearl Jam, among others. We continue to drink wine and sing and dance. I have the great idea to take off my shirt and pants and dance around in my boxers. One of the Asian girls, not Jeff's girl, gets up and strips down to her bra and panties and joins me on the dance floor, also known as, the living room floor.

Our dancing is more like hopping and flailing. Rob jumps

up, sheds his clothes, and joins us, as does the other Asian chick, not Jeff's girl. The four of us dancing around like Zen Lunatics, hopping, flailing, and smiling, without a care in the world. Jeff jumps right into another song and we continue, trying to drink wine and dance, spilling some wine on our half naked bodies. Drew is staring at Jeff's girl like a creeper and she looks at him with that why are you staring at me face. I smile and laugh out loud because I will have a personal chauffeur for a month.

"Bear!" I yell.

"Yeah!" he yells back.

"Take off your clothes and roll us some joints," I instruct.

"Will do Mad Max, will do." Bear goes to his room and comes back in his chones holding his weed purse, which he calls his briefcase, but it's a purse. He sits down and starts rolling joints. Drew has now joined us on the dance floor, in his undies of course. Jeff is still playing songs on the guitar for us and his girl is sitting next to him, both are still dressed, for now. Bear finishes rolling the joints, lights one, takes a hit, and passes it to me. We all take turns hitting the joint, which goes fast, but Bear has another one ready to rock and roll. We dance, we drink, we laugh, and we smoke, as Jeff plays the shit out of that acoustic guitar.

I tell Jeff to put down the guitar, turn on the stereo, grab his girl, and join us on the dance floor, which he does. The eight of us drinking and smoking and hopping and flailing around the living room dance floor having a grand old time.

The next thing I know, I am lying in my boxers on the kitchen floor, which is extremely cold. It is morning and my head is pounding; fucking wine. I slowly make my way to a standing position and then head into the living room. Bear and Drew and one of the Asian chicks, not Jeff's girl, are all passed out on the couch together, still in their underwear. I walk back to my room, open the door, and see Rob and the other Asian chick, not Jeff's girl, naked and passed out on my bed. I smile, shut the door, and head to Bear's room. I open the door and see Jeff and his girl, both still in their underwear, passed out on the bed. I walk back to the kitchen and start a large pot of coffee and think to myself what an unexpected great night.

A couple of hours later the four of us guys are sitting in the living room recuperating. Jeff and his three Asian Valley girls have already left. I suggest to the guys that we head down to Venice Beach and enjoy the unseasonably warm December day. Drew can't because he has to work, but Rob and Bear are down. We shower, get dressed and head out. The Venice Beach Boardwalk is a good distance from our place. But we decide to walk because driving and trying to find a parking spot is not worth the hassle. We head west down Washington Boulevard and hit a Starbucks on the way and grab a coffee and a muffin.

We reach the Ocean Front Walk and head north towards the Boardwalk. We walk past several condominiums and I tell the guys that my dream is to live in one of these places and wake up every morning and enjoy a cup of coffee on my patio, staring out at the beautiful blue Pacific Ocean. Rob tells me that dreams are good to have, but that there is no way I will ever live in one of those places. Bear asks me if he can live with me if I do end up living in one of them and I say of course.

We pass the mini-tennis courts, which are just that, tennis courts that are smaller than traditional courts. Players use paddles instead of rackets, so they might call them racket courts, but I'm not sure. Right after the courts we hit Muscle Beach, the outdoor workout gym that was made famous by Arnold Schwarzenegger. I think he worked out there during his competitive bodybuilding period, before all the action movies. Then we pass the outdoor basketball courts, where I believe they filmed parts of the movie *White Men Can't Jump*. The courts were full and five on five games were going on simultaneously.

After the basketball courts we merge to the left and head towards the skate park. This area, which is between the Ocean Front Walk and the beach, is loaded with palm trees, graffiti art and various sculptures. Venice is the Holy Land of skateboarding, along with Santa Monica, this is where it all began, almost thirty years ago. We stop and watch the skateboarders for a while. Then out of the blue Bear stands up and walks towards a kid that is waiting to drop-in to the bowl. Rob and I look at each other like, what is he doing? He talks to the kid, who looks like he is about twelve, for several seconds. Then we see the kid hand Bear his board and Bear drops-in to the bowl.

"I hope he breaks his neck," I say to Rob, who laughs.

"He looks like he knows what he's doing."

"Yeah, he's a real Dogtown maniac on a board, but it's been a while."

Bear finishes up, hands the board back to the kid, gives him a fist bump, and then heads back towards us.

"Sorry guys, had to," he says as he sits back down.

"Looked good man," Rob says.

"I'll be honest, I was hoping for a fall," I say, smiling.

"I know you were."

We head back to the Ocean Front Walk, continuing north. The Walk is a trip because you have shops on the east-side of it and artisans on the west-side of it. The shops range from souvenir shops to tattoo shops to eating establishments. The artisans are just people who set up their goods on a blanket or a fold-out table. I assume all the artisans are homeless because they look homeless, but I like their stuff anyway because it is real. Well, some of it is real garbage, but most of it is pretty cool. We jump into shops here and there and check out the artisan tables when something catches our eye. We grab a slice of pepperoni pizza and a soda and continue on, passing the Venice Beach Freak Show and more shops. When we reach the end of the Walk we take a sharp left, take off our shoes and socks, and walk across the beach sand to the Ocean.

We walk back south down the beach and at one point Bear challenges Rob and I to a foot race. He says this is where Rocky Balboa and Apollo Creed had their race in the film

Rocky III. We are not up to the challenge, so Bear runs down the beach anyway but stops after about thirty yards. He bends over at the waist breathing hard, damn pothead. We walk off the beach, get back on the Ocean Front Walk southbound, and then head back to the house.

We enjoy two more days of drinking, smoking, dancing, and sightseeing. Then I get an unexpected text message from Lacey, one of the San Diego chicks Bear and I met at Bryce Canyon a few months ago. She wanted to know if we wanted to drive down to San Diego and party and possibly spend New Year's Eve in Tijuana. After conversing with the guys, who were all down for the trip, I texted her back and told her that we would head down tomorrow, New Year's Eve. She texted me her address and I told her that we would be there around two o'clock for the pre-party.

CHAPTER NINE

We wake up the morning of New Year's Eve and pack up for our trip down to San Diego and Tijuana. The four of us load into the Jeep and head out. We stop at Tito's Tacos for an early lunch, Rob's request, and then we jump on Interstate 405 and head south. Lacey actually lives in Chula Vista, which is just south of San Diego, about a two hour drive. It is just past noon so we should be there pretty close to my estimated arrival time of two o'clock. I text Lacey and let her know that we are on our way, she texts back that she is excited to see us.

We drive through L.A County and then through Orange County until we pass the John Wayne Airport and then merge onto Interstate 5 southbound. We take Interstate 5 through San

Clemente, then Oceanside and Carlsbad, then passed the famous golf course at Torrey Pines, as we head into the city limits of San Diego.

We pull up in front of Lacey's place a little after two-thirty, because we decided to stop and grab a bottle of tequila at a liquor store down the street. We get out and walk up to the front door. Before we reach the door, Lacey opens it, runs towards us and jumps on me, giving me a huge hug. I hug her back and then look at her face, because honestly I could not remember exactly what she looked like. She could have been her friend Jen and I wouldn't have known the difference. She leads us inside and tells us to take a seat anywhere. I head to the kitchen to set the bottle of tequila down and Lacey follows me. I set the bottle down, turn around, and Lacey plants a long, hard, wet kiss on me. We separate and I'm thinking holy shit that was awesome, but I don't say it, I just smile. She smiles back, spins, and walks out of the kitchen leaving me dazed and confused.

Lacey's mother is apparently going to drop us off at the border tonight at ten and then pick us up at one in the morning. We do not want to be there any later than that, besides, three hours in Tijuana is long enough. We will continue the party when we get back to Lacey's house. She tells us that her mom has a Nissan van so we can squeeze everyone in. With the four of us guys, Lacey and her three friends, and her mom we have nine. There should be no problem cramming nine into a van. Since Lacey's mom is driving us we decide to start the party, cracking beers and smoking cigarettes out in the backyard.

Lacey tells me that she was upset that I did not try to make out with her at Bryce and that I did not call her. I told her that I wanted to but that I was exhausted from the hike that day and the night before in Vegas. I told her that I didn't call because, honestly I totally forgot that I got her number and that I was dealing with some other personal issues (a lie, sort of). She understood and told me that she got over it and thought that if she wanted to see me she would just have to take the initiative and contact me herself, which she did. She said she thought New Year's Eve in Tijuana would be a good occasion for us to visit. I told her that I would have come down just to hang out and she smiled at that.

People start to show up for the pre-party and introductions start being thrown around. We meet the three other girls that are going to be heading across the border with us, Jen was not one of them, and the guys start taking dibs on who gets who. We are still out back, music bumping, and throwing back beers and margaritas. We are having a great time, but apparently the music is too loud because the next door neighbor pokes her head over the wall and starts yelling at us.

"You need to turn that music down," the lady yells. We look over and notice the lady and I decided to walk over and take care of it.

"What was that?"

"You need to turn that damn music down. I can't hear

myself think over here."

The lady is in her early forties, white, with brown greying hair. She is wearing a night gown, which is strange because it is five o'clock in the early evening.

I reply to her request, "I'm sorry but we don't need to do anything."

"Excuse me," she yells back.

"If you would have walked over, knocked on the door, and asked us politely, we would have gladly turned the music down. But you didn't do that, you popped your head over this wall and demanded that we turn the music down. Now that is not very polite, that is not how people resolve conflict." What was I thinking trying to discuss this situation rationally with a crazy woman in a night gown?

"Screw you buddy, I'm calling the police." She starts to walk off.

"Wait, ma'am, please, come back over here and talk to me." she comes stomping back over and I try a different strategy.

"Look, its New Year's Eve, and I don't want to bother the police with a noise complaint and I don't think you want to either. So, I will personally turn the music down if you do me one favor."

She has a confused look on her face and says, "What favor?"

"I will turn down the music, but only if you go inside, put on something nice, and come over and party with us."

"What? You're crazy."

"That might be true, but that's the deal."

She cracks a tiny smile, "Are you sure I'm welcome?"

"Yes. Now go get dressed and head on over."

"Okay." She runs inside and I head back over to Lacey, who is now talking to Rob, Bear, and Drew.

"Dude, what the hell happened?" Drew asks.

"Huh? Oh I took care of it, don't worry."

"Should we be worried?" Rob asks.

"Not at all."

Bear chimes in, "so how'd you take care of it man?"

"Umm, I told her I would turn the music down but only if she came over and partied with us," I smile.

"Shut the fuck up. That lady will not come over here and party with us. She hates me," Lacey says.

"Well she's getting ready right now and should be over soon." I smile again.

"You're insane bro," Drew says.

"A fucking lunatic," adds Bear.

"And my fucking hero," Rob proclaims.

Twenty minutes later the doorbell rings and I run to answer it thinking that it is the next door neighbor lady, which it is. I welcome her in and tell her to follow me out back. She is dressed nice and I could tell she took a little time to get ready. I assume she doesn't get out much and was flattered by the invitation. We get outside and I introduce her to Lacey and the guys. I ask her if she would like a margarita, she says yes, and

I go to grab her one. I return, hand it to her, she thanks me, and takes a sip. I never turn down the music and just like I figured, she has totally forgotten about it. We all continue to enjoy the warm winter Southern California weather as well as our drinks and conversations.

At eight o'clock on the dot I head inside, grab the bottle of tequila, and several plastic cups. I head back out back and yell to the crowd, "Time for tequila shots, if you are down, come grab a cup." Several people take a cup and I fill each one with a four second pour. I raise my cup and everyone follows, even those with other drinks in their hands.

"Here's to a great night, a safe night, and a happy new year." Everyone yells and takes a drink of their respective beverage.

The party continues until it is time to make our way to the border and to Tijuana. Lacey's mom shows up and the eight of us hop in the van. The people who are not going to Mexico stay and continue to party. We will be back in three hours and rejoin the festivities, which will still be going on. The trip to the border parking lot is only fifteen minutes. When we get there, we get out, thank her for the ride, and make our way to the border entrance. I realize as we enter Mexico that one of the reasons Lacey must have called me was because she didn't want to be in Tijuana on New Year's with just her and her three friends. It can get scary especially for three hot chicks after dark. The thought quickly fades as we entered the streets of Tijuana.

We walk a block or two and enter an area off of Ave de la Amistad that looks like an outdoor shopping center. There are pharmacies and souvenir shops, and restaurants. We walk a little further and reach our destination, a huge place, called Club Fusion. Lacey says she heard about this place from a friend but she had no idea it was this big. The music from inside is bumping so loud we can not only hear it, but feel it. The cover charge is twenty bucks a piece, which includes two drinks, so it's not too bad.

We pay and enter the club and there is hardly any room to walk, but we make our way to the bar. As I try to get the bartenders attention I notice that he is only wearing thong underwear, which I find odd, but this is Mexico. I continue to wait and as I do I look around, noticing several men go-go dancing on small stages around the club. I also notice that there is an unusually large amount of muscular, well-groomed men in this place. I turn and look at the rest of the group with a bewildered look on my face.

"What's up Mad Max?" asks Drew.

"Um, I think this is a gay bar Drewski."

"What? No. How do you know?" asks Lacey.

"Well the bartender in the neon green thong was my first indication. And look around. Dudes. Everywhere."

They all look around and Lacey's friend Toni chimes in, "I think you're right."

"Yep, definitely a gay bar," adds Bear.

"You guys want to leave?" Lacey asks.

I look at Drew and Bear and they shrug their shoulders. I look at Lacey and say, "Nah fuck it we can chill for a while, but maybe in a bit we can find a different place to celebrate the New Year."

"Okay."

"And we don't have to worry about any guys hitting on you ladies so..."

"Yeah, but now we have to worry about guys hitting on you three," yells Lacey's other friend Deb.

"You don't have to worry about that," Rob yells back.

The bartender finally makes eye contact with me and nods his head. I order eight Coronas and eight shots of tequila, which came out to a whopping thirty-two U.S dollars. You have to love Mexico, shit is so cheap here. We walk over to a somewhat open spot where we can at least stretch out a little and not be right in each other's face. We raise our shot glasses, Lacey's other friend Diane says a little toast, and we drink. No salt and no lime, because that is American pussy shit. We stand and drink our beers and try to talk, but the music is blasting and we can't yell over it very well, so we stop trying. After we finish our beers I suggest to Rob, Drew, and Bear that we go grab another round, which we do, which were free. Well not free but part of our cover charge.

We return to the ladies five minutes later each holding four bottles of Corona between our fingers, two for each of us, it is double-fisting time. The ladies each take two and we start drinking. I make a suggestion that we might as well hit the

148

dance floor since we are here and the music is bumping. Everyone is down so we head to the dance floor, beers in hand, make that both hands. I am dancing with Lacey and each of the guys has chosen a girl and is dancing with them. We dance for about thirty minutes and during that time at least three guys try to cut in on our girls, not to dance with them, but with us, and they blocked them every time. We laugh hysterically. One time I push Lacey to the side and dance with some guy for a few seconds before Lacey cut back in. We laugh hysterically again.

It is eleven o'clock and we decide to leave and find a bar that is more chill to ring in the New Year. We ask around and an older Mexican guy points us in the direction of a little place called Tequila Restuarante Bar, which we literally passed when we were headed to Club Fusion a hour ago. The cover here is only ten bucks, but no free drinks. We enter and it is a quaint little place and it is pretty full, but there is still room to move around. We head to the bar and order the usual, Coronas and tequila shots. We get our drinks and Rob taps me on the shoulder.

"Dude. You are not gonna believe this."

"What's up?"

"When you told me we were going to San Diego I should have said something."

"What are you talkin' about?"

"Caroline flew down to San Diego to see her folks for Christmas."

"What does that have to do with anything? We're in Mexico, man."

"Yeah and apparently so is Caroline." Rob points across the room and as sure as shit, there she is, with her blond hair and cowboy boots. She doesn't see us and I turn away.

"Well this might get awkward. What do I do?" I ask Rob.

"Shit I don't know man. Should we leave?"

"And do what? Go back to the meat market? Nah, let me think for a sec...Who is she with?"

Rob looks towards her. "Um, it looks like a group, just like ours, a few girls and a few guys."

"Is that guy with her?"

"Um, I don't see him. Oh shit? Rob turns quickly and ducks his head.

"What?"

"I think she saw me."

"Shit, that's no bueno. Is she comin' over here?"

"I don't know. I'm too afraid to look."

At that moment we hear her voice. "Rob. Is that you?"

Rob turns around smiling. "Caroline, what the hell are you doing here?"

"I'm here with some old high school friends."

"What are you doing down here? Who are you with?"

"Um, I'm here with..." Rob turns his head towards me and I slowly turn around. "Max." Caroline's eyes get wide and a huge smile forms on her face. "Oh my god, Max," she screams for the entire bar to hear including Lacey and the rest of our party. She gives me a huge hug and I can smell her perfume and I can feel her body against mine and I don't want it to end. But it does and I immediately look over at Lacey who is giving me the, who the fuck is that bitch, look.

I act quickly. "Caroline, it's great to see you, but right now is not the greatest time to catch up. I want to talk to you but now is not the best time. So, can I call you tomorrow?"

She seems confused. "Yeah. Okay."

"Hey I just don't want to steal you away from your friends tonight, that's all, okay?"

"Yeah, I get it, it's cool." She waves bye to us and walks back over to her friends.

I turn and face our group. "Who's ready for another tequila shot?" Everyone yells, "Meeeeeee." Except for Lacey, who is staring at me with that, you better come over here and explain to me who the fuck that bitch was, look. I stay put and make her come to me, which she does a few seconds later.

"So who was that?"

"That was Rob's roommate and a friend of mine from Chico."

"Just a friend?"

"Just a friend."

We continue to drink and before we know it the clock strikes twelve. Lacey kisses me and gives me a hug.

"Happy New Year" she says.

"Happy New Year." I say, as I search the bar with my eyes, looking for Caroline.

We drink for another half an hour and then head back over the border. Lacey's mom arrives exactly at one in the morning, we hop in, and head back to Lacey's house. When we get back to the house the party is still going strong, even the neighbor lady is still there. We drink a little more, smoke a little weed and then I fall asleep with Lacey, in her bed, but nothing happens. After we wake up, we say our goodbyes and leave. We decide to grab some breakfast at a nearby local breakfast joint before we head back up to L.A. Three hours later we are sitting in our living room. I pick up my phone and call Caroline.

"Hi," she says.

"Hey."

"So what's up?"

"Well, first I want to say that it was great seeing you last night and I'm sorry if I was short with you but I was with someone and I didn't want to deal with any drama."

"I understand. Are you two serious?

"No, no, no. Bear and I met her and her friend at Bryce Canyon a few months ago and that was the first time I had seen her since. I don't expect to see her again. So how's life?"

"Life is good."

"How's the student teaching going?"

"It's going good. I start my real student teaching in three weeks when the spring semester starts and then in four months I will be a certified teacher."

"That's awesome. I'm happy for you."

"So, I've written a few poems since your visit."

"Really? That's cool. I would love to hear them some day. Well, I have go, Rob is getting hungry and he needs to get on the road, so I will talk to you later."

We say goodbye and hang up. Rob looks at me. "Well that didn't sound awkward or anything."

"I don't even know why I called her."

"You know why, but anyway, I am hungry, you mentioned food before my drive home?"

"Tito's?"

Rob Smiles. "You read my mind Mad Max."

"Alright, let's go." The four of us leave and go eat. After that we say our goodbyes and then Rob takes off north back to Chico.

CHAPTER TEN

Four months later, in early May, I contemplate getting out
of town for a while and I decide to fly to Sioux Falls and see
my father and his family. I have been miserable since my New
Year's Day conversation with Caroline and I have not talked to
her since. I call my father and he tells me to come on out and
that he will pick me up at the airport. I decide to book a one
way flight because I might end up renting a car and driving
back to L.A. I have never seen the beauty of South Dakota and
Wyoming and I have always wanted to. A week later I hop on
a Southwest 737 plane to Sioux Falls, making one stop in
Denver. I arrive as the sun sets to the west and my father is
there waiting for me. I shake his hand and we catch up as we

head to the car and then to his house.

When we get to the house, Paula, my father's wife and Brittany, their seventeen year old daughter are in the kitchen. Paula is working on dinner and Brittany is grabbing plates and silverware to set the table. Steven, their fourteen year old son is playing a video game in the living room. After we all exchange pleasant hellos I take my pack to the basement where I will be sleeping.

When I head back up dinner is ready and we sit down to eat. My father's family is a typical middle class white suburban family living in a four bedroom, three bathroom house complete with the stereotypical white picket fence. Paula is a stay at home mother who also sells Mary Kay on the side. Steven is a three sport athlete and Brittany is the captain of the cheer squad at their high school. To these people I am a fucking weirdo, but to me they are exactly why I live the way I do. I hate this cookie cutter, fake, plastic, *Leave It to Beaver* bullshit but I smile when I am here and appreciate their hospitality. They are good people, they are just boring to me and I feel sorry for them, sometimes.

"So Max, how is the writing going?" my father asks.

"It's going well. I finally started my first novel a couple of months ago."

"That is great. What is it about," Paula inquires.

"Um, it's about a guy and a girl. You know a typical love story."

"That sounds nice," says Paula.

"Is it a true story?" my father asks.

"Um, not really. I mean its fiction, but there might me a little fact in there somewhere."

The kids are not participating in the conversation, they are busy eating and texting. These kids run the show here, no discipline, which drives me crazy. I just want to yell at them to put the fucking phones away while we eat, damn rude ass teenagers.

"So how long you planning on staying?" Paula asks.

"Only a couple of days. I think I am going to rent a car and drive back to L.A."

"Really? Why is that?" my father asks.

"I just need a little me time. You know to clear my head and think about things. Plus, I've never been to Mount Rushmore or the Grand Tetons so I thought I would take this opportunity to check them out."

"Wow that sounds like a fun adventure," Paula says.

"Yeah. It should be pretty cool."

We finish eating and the kids leave, Steven back to his video game and Brittany to her room. I guess they don't feel the need to help clean up after dinner so the three of us do it. After we clear off the table, put away the leftovers, and load the dishwasher we head to the family room and chat some more while enjoying a bottle of wine. We finish the bottle and open another. Thirty minutes later we head to bed.

I stay up for about an hour, in the basement, writing a poem and thinking about Caroline. She has been with that guy for eight months, which means it must be pretty serious. I contemplate just telling her how I feel, but I keep thinking about the guy. What if I was in his shoes and I was with Caroline and some dude just walked up and told her that he loved her and that she should drop me and be with him? I mean that is some fucked up shit, but on the other side, what if she loves me and doesn't know how I feel because I haven't told her? Love sucks. I just need to get on the road and figure it all out.

I wake up to the smell of bacon coming from upstairs and make my way to the kitchen. Paula is slaving away making a huge breakfast that includes, pancakes, eggs, country potatoes, bacon, and biscuits with white gravy. She tells me to grab a plate and load it up, which I do. I take some of everything and take a seat at the dining room table. My father enters the kitchen and grabs a plate.

"Sleep alright?" he asks.

"Yeah, the pull-out was not too bad."

"So what's the plan?"

"Well, I know I've only been here a day, but I think I'm gonna take off tomorrow morning."

"Okay, that's fine. It is a long drive back to L.A."

"It sure is. So father?"

"Yes son."

"Think you can give me a lift to the rental car place today so I can grab a car?"

"No."

"No?"

"Well Paula and I were talking last night and she suggested that I let you take the Mustang."

"What's that? The Mustang? Your baby?"

Paula jumps in, "That thing just sits in the garage. He hardly ever drives it. It needs to get out into the fresh air."

"She's right and it is warm enough now that you can drive her with the top down, which will make your trip home way better."

"Are you serious?"

"Yeah, but don't get too attached because I plan on visiting you this summer and driving it back here."

"Really? That's cool."

"Yeah, Paula told me I could, so I jumped at the chance."

"Well I appreciate it, thanks."

"No problem, just don't crash it."

"Don't worry, I won't."

The next morning Paula makes another great breakfast and I fill my stomach to capacity. My father leads me to the garage, pulls the cover off of the Mustang, and gives me the keys. The Mustang is a 1967, two-door, convertible, royal blue and it is in pristine condition. I have wanted to drive this car for years, every time I come to visit. I go back inside, pack, say my goodbyes, and head out, back west, excited for what is to come.

The drive west on Interstate 90 through South Dakota is long and boring. The landscape is pretty flat with beautiful green and gold rolling hills and a sky so blue is looks like an impressionist painting. This is what I see for over two hundred and fifty miles. Beautiful? Yes, but still boring. I exit the interstate and take a left onto Highway 240 and head south towards Badlands National Park. The highway makes a turn back west and as I make my way through the Badlands I wonder how these rock formation are even here. It is like they just sprung up out of the ground like the structures at Monument Valley. They look like the wind and rain eroded formations at Bryce Canyon, but they are not an orange tan color, but more of a greyish tan color, more than likely because they are different layers of the Earth's crust.

I stop a couple of times to stretch and to soak in the scenery. I take time to close my eyes and meditate in one of the most beautiful landscapes in America. I bet this is what the first Native Americans who came into this area thought and I wish I could go back in time and talk with them. I open my eyes and realize that I have gone back in time, the Badlands look the same today as they did thousands of years ago. I head back to Interstate 90 for the short drive to the Black Hills.

Forty minutes later I reach Rapid City and stop for gas and a bite to eat, then I head south on Highway 16 into the Black Hills towards Mount Rushmore. I take a left on Highway 16A twenty-five minutes later and then I take a right onto Highway 244. I park in the Mount Rushmore parking lot fifteen minutes later and walk up to check it out. As I make my way up the walkway to the Monument I pass under all of the flags of the

United States that are flapping above. I get to the end of the walkway and there they are, the four Presidents, Washington, Jefferson, Teddy Roosevelt, and Honest Abe.

They are farther away than I thought they would be and it is not as amazing as pictures I have seen. There are a ton of tourists here and I have had enough; I don't like to be around this many people. Besides this place is kind of disrespectful, I mean, the U.S. government decided to carve the faces of four white American Presidents into one of the most sacred mountain ranges in Native American culture, what the fuck?

I get back in the Mustang and head out of the Black Hills, which are really more grey than black, but they are beautiful and I can see why the Natives consider them so spiritual. I exit the Black Hills and reach the Wyoming border an hour later. I hit the town of Newcastle shortly after and head north on Highway 85. Twenty minutes later I arrive in the town of Four Corners and take a left on Highway 585 and continue heading north. I reach the town of Sundance twenty-five miles later and jump back on Interstate 90, but only for two miles. I exit the Interstate and head north on Highway 14 towards my next stop, Devil's Tower National Monument. Twenty-five minutes later I continue heading north, now on Highway 24 and reach Devil's Tower, which blows my mind.

Devil's Tower is basically a rock protrusion like the ones at Monument Valley except there is just one in the middle of nowhere, it is grey, not orange, and there are trees around it. It is insane and I am totally mesmerized by this thing. I decide to camp here for the night so I can absorb the spiritualness of this awesome rock formation and wake up to it staring at me. I grab my pack and head towards the Tower looking around for any government officials that might kick me out of here. I don't see any as I make my way closer to the formation.

I hike around to the other side of it so no one will see me and I find a nice spot to camp for the night. The weather is unseasonably warm, which is good for me, but it will still be cool tonight and I am glad I brought my cold weather sleeping bag. I set up my sleeping gear and climb inside my sleeping bag as the sun sets. As I lay here looking at the stars I think about Caroline and how great it would be if she were here with me. I hope one day I can come back with her, but I am still conflicted with what to do, so I meditate on it, hoping for a sign from somewhere.

I feel the sun on my face as I awake and open my eyes. I look up and Devil's Tower is still there and I smile; what an amazing way to wake up. I lay there for a bit and soak it all in before packing up and heading back to the Mustang. When I get to the car I turn and look at Devils Tower one last time and I hope I will have a chance to see it again. I head south on Highway 24 and then Highway 14 back towards Interstate 90, which I hit thirty minutes later.

After a ninety-five mile drive I enter the town of Buffalo, Wyoming, a small town at the base of the Bighorn National Forest. I stop for gas and then hit up a local cafe for some breakfast. I eat a short stack of pancakes with a side of bacon and three cups of coffee. After I finish eating I get back on the road and I jump on Highway 16, which cuts and winds through the Bighorn National Forest. The forest is lush with trees and the mountain peaks are majestic. An hour later I am almost through the Forest when I see an amazing view and I decide to pull over and check it out. I get out and I see Meadowlark Lake and the rest of central Wyoming to the southwest. The view is spectacular and I am glad I stopped to check it out. A few minutes later I get back on the highway and head west towards Yellowstone Park, which is still four hours away.

I hit the city of Worland and take a right onto Highway 789 and head north. Thirty-five minutes later I take a left onto Highway 16 and head west, which will take me all the way to Yellowstone. I drive through the city of Cody and pass the Buffalo Bill Reservoir and Dam as I enter the Shoshone National Forest. I pass Cody Peak and then reach Yellowstone Lake, a massive body of water in the eastern section of the park. At the northern part of the lake I take a left and head south on Highway 20, which hugs the western shore of the lake. Twenty minutes later I reach Highway 191.

At this point I can continue on Highway 20, which will take me to Old Faithful, and then I can head back to Highway 191 and continue on to the Grand Tetons or I can just head to the Tetons. I decide to just head to the Tetons and bypass Old Faithful because I don't think looking at a hole in the ground that shoots water into the sky is worth the time it would take and there are probably a millions tourists there. So I head south on Highway 191, passing Jackson Lake to the right, and then I take a right onto Teton Park Road.

As I drive towards Jenny Lake, my stop for the night, I see several buffalo roaming free and snacking on the wild grasses of the park. I have seen buffalo before but not like this, not free roaming without any fences, it was nice to see. I pull into the Jenny Lake Campground and find a campsite to claim as mine for the night. Jenny Lake is a small lake at the base of the Grand Tetons. When I get out of the car I am in awe, the Grand Tetons are right in front of my face and they are glorious. They are dark grey and craggily, they look like the Alps, which I have only seen in pictures, complete with snowcapped peaks, which are hidden by thin, elongated clouds. The air up here is so crisp and clean and I take a deep breath, something I would never do in L.A. I am just going to stay at the campsite tonight so I leave the car, my Camelback pack in hand, and head towards the small boat launch.

I decide to take the ten dollar ferry across the lake to the trailhead instead of hiking it so I will have time to hike up Cascade Canyon before dark. I jump on the ferry, which is really just a silver motor boat that can hold about thirty people or so. After the short trip across the lake, I get off the boat and head up the trail to Hidden Falls. The falls are above the trail and are about two hundred feet high with tall green trees on either side of it.

It is getting warmer out and the melting ice has the falls

flowing pretty good. I continue on the trail to Inspiration
Point, a viewpoint that allows me to see Jenny Lake and
hundreds of miles of western and central Wyoming beyond it.
After a few minutes of inspiration I continue on the trail west
through Cascade Canyon. The canyon trail is a dirt trail with
green brush and trees on either side of it and grey craggily
mountains beyond that. The snow on the peaks cool me down
as the wind blows and I make my way up through the canyon.

I want to continue on but I have head back to catch the
ferry. If I miss the ferry I will have to make the three and a
half mile hike around the southern shore of the lake, which I
would if it was earlier. I really don't like hiking in the dark and
I don't think I could make it anyway, the altitude is starting to
get to me. I make it back to the ferry, which takes me back to
the other side of the lake and my campsite as the sun sets
beyond the Grand Tetons, which I remember are part of the
Rocky Mountain Range.

I got back to my campsite, set up my sleeping gear, and
climbed inside my sleeping bag. It has been a long day, shit a
long couple of days, shit a long couple of months, and I need
some rest. I think about Caroline for a bit and try not to think
about her with her guy friend. I think about Drew and Bear
and wonder what kind of shenanigans they are getting into. I
think about my life and if I am doing it right, if I'm living up
to whatever I am supposed to be doing with it. I think, is God
disappointed in me? Are my parents disappointed in me? Are
my friends disappointed in me? Are my college professors

disappointed in me? Is Caroline disappointed in me?

Sometimes I think I should just go to teacher school and get a "real" job teaching high school English like Caroline, a respectable job that everyone will be proud of. But then I realize that this is my life, not theirs, and if I want to spend my life wandering around and writing and partying and enjoying what this country has to offer, then that is what I am going to do. And if God or my parents or my friends or my professors don't like it, well to hell with them, even though I love them all very much.

I fall asleep under a billion stars that float in the immense dark sky above, with the Grand Tetons staring at me, and it is peaceful. I awake ten hours later to the grandeur that is the Grand Tetons and I lie there for a while as the sun rises behind me. All I hear is nature's symphony of unseen insects and winds blowing through the trees, making the branches and leaves dance like they were drunk on wine.

I finally get up, pack, and head out. I jump back on Teton Park Road and head south. I reach Highway 191 and continue south to the city of Jackson where I stop for some breakfast. After a hearty meal I continue the drive south on Highway 191 towards Interstate 80 and the Utah border. An hour later I stay to the right and continue south through southwestern Wyoming, now on Highway 189. I reach the town of Kemmerer an hour and a half later and then Interstate 80 thirty-five minutes after that. Forty minutes later I hit Interstate 84 just east of Salt Lake City and take it south and then west to Interstate 15, which I will take basically all the way home to L.A. But as fate would have it, I get a call from Rob, and my plans change.

In Salt Lake City you have four options out of town, the way I just came, north on Interstate 15 to Idaho, south on Interstate 15 to Southern Nevada and Southern California, or west on Interstate 80 to Northern Nevada and Northern California. Rob calls me at this moment, before I have to merge onto Interstate 15 and head home.

"Mad Max. What is up?"

"Nothin' man just drivin' back from Sioux Falls. What are you doin'?"

"Nothin'. Where are you right now?"

"Just hit Salt Lake City, about to jump on the 15 and head home."

"Any chance you can make a detour and head here?"

"To Chico? Do you really want to see me that bad bro?"

"Well, I always want to see you man, but this isn't about me."

"Well, what's it about then?"

"Caroline."

"What about her?"

"She just told me that her and her boyfriend split up last night."

My heart begins to pump at an incredible rate and I get the chills. "So what am I supposed to do?"

"Get your ass here and tell her how you feel man. You

166

didn't want to do it because she had a boyfriend, well now she doesn't. So grow some balls, get your ass here, and tell her."

I am two miles away from Interstates 15 and 80 and I don't have time to think about it, which is probably a good thing. I have to make a decision, one that might change my life forever.

"Well, I guess I have to give it shot man. You can't live life on what ifs."

"Yes, that's what I'm talkin' about."

I merge onto Interstate 80 and head west towards northern Nevada.

"So what's the plan?" Rob asks.

"I don't know man, let me think about it and I will call you back."

"Sounds good man. Talk to ya later."

"Hey Rob?"

"Yeah."

"You're sure it's over between them?"

"As of right now it is. Just get here quick man."

"Alright, I'll call you in a bit."

"Cool, see ya."

My mind is racing and all these thoughts and emotions are bouncing around in my skull as I drive along the southern shore of the Great Salt Lake. I have ten hours to think about it, which is way too long to think about something, especially something like this. As I cross into Nevada I think I have a plan and I call Rob before the reception gets shitty. I tell him my plan and he loves it, now all I have to do is get there and find the courage to say what I want to say.

I stop in the town of Elko, Nevada for gas, smokes, and energy drinks. I can't eat so I skip the snacks. After four hours of some of the most boring scenery I have ever experienced, I reach Reno. It is dark out now and the closer I get to Chico the more nervous I get. The plan will be going down in the morning, so I call a buddy of mine who lives in Roseville, just east of Sacramento, and ask if I can crash on his couch for the night. He is cool with it and I reach his place an hour and a half later. We chat for a little while, but he can tell my mind is elsewhere, which it is, so he heads to bed and I fall asleep on the couch. I wake up early and tell my buddy it was good to see him and I thank him for his hospitality. I hit the road and head north on Highway 99, Chico is only ninety miles away.

I park and head out to the spot where I plan on telling Caroline how I feel. I am about a half an hour early, which is stressing me out, I just want to get it over with. Finally, I see two people walking towards me and my heart begins to race, but it turns out that it is not them and I take a deep breath and exhale. As the couple passes me we smile at each other. At that moment I look up and I see two people standing in the distance. I can't really make out their faces but I know it is Rob and Caroline.

I see Rob turn and walk away and Caroline begins to walk towards me. As she gets closer my heart is beating out of my chest and my palms are all sweaty. She is in a yellow sun dress that makes her blend into the scenery around her. She is also wearing her cowboy boots, which drive me crazy. Her blond hair is long and curly and shining in the sunlight. She finally gets close enough to recognize me and I see her and she is more beautiful than the wildflowers that surround us.

"Max?"

"Hey Caroline."

"What's going on? I'm slightly confused. Rob just told me to come with him and that he wanted to show me something."

"I told him to bring you here."

"Why?"

"A year ago you brought me here, twice, and I've never forgotten it. Every day since I have thought about you. When you told me that you had met someone I lied and said I was happy for you but I wasn't. For the past eight months I have wanted to tell you how much you mean to me, but I didn't want to mess with your relationship. So when Rob called me yesterday and told me that you two broke up I made a detour and came right here. I don't know how this is going to turn out but I just need to tell you that I love you. And I need you and I want you and I don't want to wake up another day without you next to me. I want to lie down on every roof in the world with you and look up at the stars. I want to kiss you under every waterfall that exists. I want to experience life with you and hold you and..."

"Max," she interrupts.

"Yeah."

"It's about fucking time." A tear runs down her left cheek and she smiles. "Now shut up and kiss me." I smile back and kiss her with all the passion I have in my mind, body, and soul. We walk back to the Mustang through the wildflowers, holding hands, both smiling ear to ear. Rob has left. He is such an optimist.

"Nice car, is this new?"

"No, it's my fathers. It's just a loaner. I drove it here from Sioux Falls." We get into the car, the top is down.

"You drove all the way here from South Dakota?"

"Yeah, it's a long story, which I can tell you over lunch?"

"I would love some lunch. I am starving." She looks at me and smiles and I smile back. I put the car in reverse and back out onto the road. I then put the car in drive and head back to Chico. Caroline grabs my right hand and intertwines her fingers with mine and we smile.

"So, are you going to teach me how to be a Zen Lunatic?"

"You can't teach Zen lunacy, we all have it inside of us, you just have to find it."

"Will you help me find it then?"

I look at her and smile. "I will help you find it."

I love you and miss you dad.

(T.A. Maxwell Sr. 1954-2012)

About the Author

T.A. Maxwell was born in Southern California.
He is the father of one son and one daughter.
His current whereabouts are unknown.
This is his first novel.

Also by T.A. Maxwell

I Am Joe American and Other Poems
Broken Like Vinyl
On the Road to Big Blackfoot
Into The Ocean
Sexy, Smart, Crazy Beautiful

The Following Pages Contain a Sneak Peak
of T.A. Maxwell's Sequel to The Zen Lunatics:

On The Road to Big Blackfoot

❀

"I need to go to Flagstaff." I say to my friend and
roommate Bear as I hit the end call button on my cellphone.
We were enjoying a relaxing Thursday afternoon lounging
around the house, eating unhealthy cereal, smoking a little
weed, and watching a Man vs. Food marathon on the Travel
Channel when I got a call from my father.

"Oh yeah. When?" Bear asks.

"Like tomorrow."

"Oh yeah. Why is that?"

"My father has cancer." Saying that seemed so surreal and
I could not believe that those words had passed through my
lips. I look at Bear and he looks back at me. I could tell he was

searching his vocabulary bank to find the right words to respond to what I had just said.

"What kind?" This was what he had come up with.

"What do you mean?" I could not really grasp the question, even though I knew what he meant.

"What kind of cancer? Where is it?"

"Oh." I said as I shook away the imaginary cobwebs that had quickly developed in my head. "Brain cancer. That's all he said. I have brain cancer."

Bear shakes his head and comes back with "that sucks man."

"Yep, it sure does." We sit there in the living room of our three bedroom house in Venice, California, in our underwear, both shaking our heads back and forth like a couple of bobblehead dolls.

Bear and I have been roommates for two years now, but it has only been a few months that we have lived together without our other friend and roommate Max. He moved out four months ago and headed up to Seattle with his new girlfriend Caroline. They both found jobs teaching English, he, at a high school and she, at a middle school. Bear and I have become pretty close these past couple of month's but we are still different people and deal with things differently. He is more relaxed and pretty much has a whatever attitude about everything. I am more on edge and tend to freak out when things go all crazy. The weed helps but it's not the cure all.

"I need to figure out how I'm gettin' to Flag."

"Plane?" Bear suggests.

"Shit, a last minute flight will cost an arm and a leg,

besides, it is not like he's on his death bed, I don't need to get there in a couple hours, more like a day or two. What about a bus?"

"Yeah, a bus will definitely be cheaper."

"Can you look online for schedules, ticket prices and shit while I look for my pack and start packing?"

"Of course man, you go pack and I'll find you a ride out of town."

"Thanks Bear." I stand up and head to my room to search for my pack. My mind is still racing as I repeat, in my head, the quick conversation my father and I just had not ten minutes ago.

"Hello."

"Hey Andrew. It's your father. How ya been?"

"Not too bad. You?"

"Well, that's sort of why I'm calling. I'm not doin' great."

"What's goin' on?"

"Well, it appears that I have brain cancer son."

"What?"

"I have brain cancer. Can you come see me? I need to see you. We need to talk."

"Yeah, I'll get there as soon as I can."

"No rush, but in the next day or two would be great."

"Okay dad, I'll see ya."

"Bye son."

Finding my pack has turned out to be a lot more difficult than I had imagined. The only place it could be is in my closet, but after throwing everything out and onto my bed, it's nowhere to be seen.

"Hey Bear, have you seen my pack?" I yell out.

"Nope, I haven't seen it since we did that weekend Yosemite hike with Max before he took off to Seattle."

"Well shit." I say so only I can hear it.

"Oh hey, I bet it's in Max's old room. Remember we put a bunch of shit in there after he left?" Bear yells back.

I smile, knowing that he is right and that is exactly where it is. The memory of throwing it in there returns as quick as it left. I exit my room and head towards Max's old room. "I bet you're right." I yell to Bear as I make my way down the hall.

"I bet I am too."

I walk in, search around for a few seconds and find it hiding in a corner of the room under a poster of the late great Johnny Cash. I grab it and head to the living room.

"You were right my brotha. The man in black was keepin' it safe."

"What?"

"Nothin'. So what's the damage on the bus fare?"

"L.A. to Flagstaff, leaving tomorrow, looks like it's gonna be eighty-five bucks."

"That's not too bad."

"Not at all. But hey I also looked on this rideshare site I go to sometimes and I found a guy who is leaving town in a couple days, headed to Colorado. He's just looking for someone to throw in for some gas. I bet you could get to Flag for forty bucks and get there faster."

"Oh yeah. But what if he's a crazy bastard or a serial killer or something?"

"Take a knife."

I laugh. "Alright email him and if he responds and takes forty I'll do it."

"Right on. It's about time for another Zen lunatic road trip." Bear says and immediately regrets. "Sorry man, I guess it's not."

"No man, it's cool, I could use a little lunacy right now."

Bear emails a message to the guy saying that I need a ride to Flagstaff to see my dying father thinking that maybe he will take me for cheaper or maybe even for free. I head back to my room and survey my clothes and pick out what I'm going to take with me. I suddenly realize that I have no idea how long I am going to be there so I pack as much as I can cram into my sixty liter pack. I decide to give the rideshare guy until the morning to reply to Bear's email. If he doesn't, then I will just head to the Greyhound bus station and buy a ticket to Flagstaff.

The next morning I wake up to the sultry sounds of Bear singing in the shower. I lay in bed for a few minutes thinking about the phone conversation I had with my father yesterday and still can't believe it. I lost my mother six years ago when I was twenty-two, after she succumbed to injuries she received after her car was t-boned by an elderly lady who had ran a red light. And now the thought of losing my other parent was thrown right in front of my face, even though the situation is a little bit different.

My parents divorced when I was eight and my mother wanted to leave Phoenix and head back to Southern California where she was born and raised. She hated Arizona, especially the heat, and she was tired of looking at nothing but the color beige or tan or sand or whatever other shades of brown there are. My father was reluctant to allow her to leave the state and take me with her, but he realized that he was the one that forced her to move to Phoenix and he felt like it was something he should do. Besides, he had ended the marriage and he figured it was the least he could do. But he did insist on being able to have me visit more often and at her expense. She agreed to let me visit two months in the summer, during my fall and spring breaks, and the week in-between Christmas and New Year's Day. As I got older though the visits decreased because I played sports and I needed to be at practice and at games during my fall and spring breaks and during parts of the summer. I usually saw him at Christmas time and a few weeks during the summer.

When I got to high school I quit playing sports but I told my father that I was still playing them so I didn't have to visit him. By this time he had moved up to Flagstaff, Arizona. It wasn't that I didn't want to see him, we just really didn't have anything in common and I was busy with school and friends and girls and I just didn't see the point.

When I turned eighteen I was not legally required to visit him anymore so I didn't. We talked on the phone now and again over the next year or so but that was pretty much it. He tried contacting me several time after that but I made no effort and I guess he just stopped trying. As I lay here, a twenty-eight year old man, I suddenly realize that I haven't seen my father in ten years and I have no idea who he is or what he might look like.

I notice the singing and the shower has stopped as I slowly

rise out of bed. At that moment Bear throws open my bedroom door. He is wearing nothing but a towel…on his head.

"Hey Drewski guess what?"

"Jesus man, put some pants on."

"I will in a sec, guess what?"

"What?"

"Rideshare guy messaged me back."

"No shit. What did he say?"

"He said he's leaving tomorrow morning and he can definitely give you a ride to Flagstaff for fifty bucks."

"Fifty huh? I guess that's better than eighty-five."

"Yeah and you don't have to stop to drop off and pick up people every twenty miles."

"Alright, email him back and tell him it sounds good."

"Cool." Bear turns and starts to walk down the hall.

"Oh and give him my number so we can talk and work out the details." I yell.

"You got it buddy" he yells back as he walks down the hall to his room to hopefully put some pants on.

I give my father a quick call to tell him that I will be there tomorrow but there is no answer so I leave a message on his answering machine. Then I grab my towel and head to the bathroom to shower. I don't sing as the hot shower water pelts my body. I try to remember the last time I saw my father, what he looked like, what we talked about, and what we did.

I remember that it was the day after Christmas and that I stayed with him until New Year's Eve morning because I had big plans that night with some buddies of mine. I remember that it had snowed a few days before I had arrived. The roads were clear but most of the town, the trees, and the mountains were covered with snow. I hated snow and cold weather, which was another reason I didn't visit that much or not at all after that winter. My father was forty-seven years old at the time. I know this because I was seventeen and he was almost exactly thirty years older than me. We were both born in the month of June.

I remember he was young looking for his age and hardly had any grey in his hair or wrinkles on his face. He was taller than me by a good half foot and still probably is. I apparently got my height from my mother's side of the family. I cannot remember what we talked about or what we did but I do remember an argument we had. He wanted to take me snowboarding at the Arizona Snow Bowl and I refused. Like I said, I hated the snow and the cold and even though it was snowboarding and that I'm sure I would have had a blast I was just over it, over everything that had to do with that place, and over him. As I think back, as the bathroom turns into a steam room, I realize that I refused to do a lot of things with my father, things that any son would have loved to do, things like fishing, hiking, kayaking, and even geocaching, which is like a nature treasure hunt. I suddenly realize that I had so much animosity towards my father for divorcing my mother that I missed out on a lot of good, fun times with him and I was instantly pissed off at myself.

I turn the shower off and throw open the shower curtain. I grab the towel that I had hung over the shower curtain rod right before I entered the shower and begin to dry off my face and hair. The bathroom is filled with so much steam it's hard to see and even breathe. I almost trip on the toilet as I step out of the shower and onto the rug on the floor. At that moment Bear opens the door, letting in a rush of cold air that hits me like an avalanche.

"What the fuck man!" I yell as I try to cover my naked body with my towel to block the cold and Bear's eyes from my private business.

"What? Just wanted to let you know that rideshare guy called your cell phone and left a message."

"Thanks man but that could have waited til I got out of the shower."

"You are out of the shower."

"The bathroom then, you know what I mean."

"Yeah, yeah." Bear says as he closes the door. The bathroom is instantly warmer and I finish drying off. I head to my room, put on some clothes, and then grab my cellphone, which is charging in the living room. I call the rideshare guy, whose name is Bill, and I learn that he's a thirty-seven year old single white guy who is on his way to Colorado to camp and kayak. We agree on the fifty dollar fee for the ride to Flagstaff and he agrees to pick me up at our place at eight tomorrow morning.

When I hang up with Bill I head back to my bedroom to finish packing and make sure I have everything I need. Then I head to the living room to hang out with Bear. We decided to invite some friends over to drink some beer and wine and hopefully get a good game of dirty Jenga going, which happens several times. It is a good send off and I hit the sack around one in the morning and set the alarm for six hours later.

The alarm sounds and I hit the snooze button not once but twice. When it sounds that super annoying sound for the third time I lean over and turn it off and finally crawl out of bed, still slightly intoxicated. I quickly head to the kitchen and start a pot of coffee and then head to the bathroom to grab a couple ibuprofen tablets for my aching head. I head back to the kitchen and fill a glass with filtered water from the pitcher in the refrigerator. I toss the two pills into my mouth and then drink the entire glass of water to make sure they go down and dissolve as quickly as possible. The coffee is still not done so I decided to take a quick shower to wake up. After showering I get dressed and then head back to the kitchen to load up on caffeine. As it gets closer to eight I check my pack and make sure I have everything I need, which I do. Then I have a seat on the living room couch and sip my third cup of coffee and wait.

When the clock hits eight I decide to grab my pack and head outside to wait for my ride. I contemplate waking Bear up and saying goodbye but decide not to because he won't remember anyway. As I open the front door I notice a four door black truck pull up right in front of our place, perfect timing on both our parts. I wave and Bill waves and then exits the truck and walks towards me.

"Hey Bill." I extend my right hand.

"Hey Drew, nice to meet you." He extends his right hand and we shake. "I made some room behind the passenger seat for your bag." He says as he walks over to the right side of his truck and I follow.

"I appreciate it."

Bill opens the rear passenger door, takes my pack from me, sets it on the back seat, and then shuts the door. "You ready to hit the road?"

"Yes sir." I say as I reach into my front pants pocket, grab the fifty dollars from my money clip, and hand it to him.

"Oh. Yeah. Thanks." He says as he takes the money and shoves it into his front right pants pocket, not bothering to count it. We head to our respective doors, open them, and climb in. Bill starts up the truck and we take off down the road. We jump on Interstate 10 and head east through Los Angeles.

"So what's in Colorado if you don't mind me asking?" I ask as I look out the passenger side window at the crowded city as the sun rises.

"Lakes."

I turn my head and look at him, "Lakes?"

"Yep, lakes. I'm headed to Colorado to kayak several lakes. Nighthorse, Electra, Crystal, Ridgeway, Blue Mesa, and a couple others."

"I guess that explains the kayak attached to the roof of your truck."

"Yep. I've been planning this trip for over a year."

"Why Colorado?"

"Well I love kayaking lakes surrounded by mountains, it's insanely beautiful. And I have family in Boulder that I'm going to visit when I'm done."

"Wow, sounds like a great trip."

"Yeah it should be pretty amazing."

We merge onto the 210 freeway and continue east towards

Pasadena. Bill continues to tell me about his trip and then he starts talking about his life. He tells me he was born in Denver, Colorado and spent most of his childhood there. After middle school his family moved to Boulder, a town just northwest of Denver, when his father was transferred there by his work.

After high school he moved to Northern California and attended UC Berkeley. He graduated five years later and took a job at a software company in Southern California, where he has been working and living ever since. He never married but was engaged once and has no children. He is currently single and not in any hurry to meet someone. He hates his job and wants to become a writer, which he might do, sooner than later.

We jump on Interstate 15 and head north towards Barstow. I can tell he wants to ask me about my father, but doesn't know how. I wait patiently for it, because I know it's coming, and it does sooner than later.

"So what's the status on your father if you don't mind me asking?" He finally says, reluctantly.

"All I know is that he has brain cancer. Not sure how bad it is or how long he's had it. He called me a couple days ago, told me he had it, asked me to come see him, so here I am."

"Brain cancer. Shit man I'm sorry. That sucks."

"Yeah it does."

"Are you guys close?"

"I haven't seen him in ten years. Shit, that was the first time I had talked with him in eight years now that I think about it."

"I take it your parents aren't together anymore?"

"Nope. Divorced when I was eight. My mother passed away six years ago."

"Damn, I'm sorry man."

"Shit happens. We have no control over any of it. When we're supposed to go, we go."

"That's true."

We reach Barstow and after stopping for a restroom break and grabbing a drink at a roadside gas station we merge onto Interstate 40 and head east towards the California/Arizona border. Flagstaff is only five hours away. As we leave Barstow behind, Bill starts up a new conversation, even though I would rather not, but I don't want to be rude.

"So what line of work are you in Drew?"

"Retail." Bill doesn't respond and I get the feeling that my short response offended him so I elaborate. "I work at a grocery store."

"Oh yeah. You like it?"

"It's okay. It pays the bills."

"No college?" I don't respond quickly enough. "I apologize. That was out of line. I didn't mean that to imply anything."

"Nah it's cool. I started college but my mother passed away during my junior year and I just never finished. I do pretty well though at my job, money is decent, and it's low stress, so it's all good."

"Well, I am a perfect example of a college degree not meaning a damn thing."

"What do you mean?"

"Well like I told you earlier I hate being a software

engineer and I'm about to give it up. That's what this trip is really about. It's my vision quest, my spiritual walkabout. I want to travel and write, which makes my degree garbage."

"That's awesome man, good for you." I smile because Bill reminds me of Max, who always talks about taking vision quests and going on spiritual walkabouts, but then I start to feel sad because I miss that damn Zen lunatic. "So what happened? What made you decide to become a writer?" I say to distract me from my sad thoughts.

"I had an epiphany one day. I was in a lousy relationship. I wasn't happy at work. I didn't have any real friends. And I didn't have the relationship I wanted to have with my family." I look at Bill and I can see tears welling up in his eyes. "So I started to reevaluate my life and tried to figure out what was important and what I needed to do to be happy. I eventually came up with a mantra I guess you can say. Three things that I needed to do to be happy."

"And those are?"

"To be happy I believe people need to love three things. One, you have to love yourself, inside and out. Two, you have to love other people, your friends, your family, your significant other, etcetera. And finally, you have to love what you do, for work and for pleasure."

I think about what Bill just said for a few seconds. "I like that man and I agree with it completely."

"It's a lot of hard work to change those things, but I think it's what we have to do to be happy. I mean how can you not be happy if you love yourself, other people, and your job?"

"Man there is no way you wouldn't be happy if you had all

that love flowing through you." I add.

As we drive over the Colorado River and enter Arizona the conversation has ceased and what Bill said a short while ago about love is bouncing around in my head. Do I love myself? I think so. I mean I'm in decent shape and I'm not a bad looking guy. I also like my personality. I don't think I annoy people and I believe I'm a good friend. Do I love what I do? Well I wouldn't say I love my job but it's fulfilling and I don't really have any complaints. And when it comes to pleasure I love writing poetry, and partying, and hiking, and just being a Zen lunatic. Do I love other people? Well I love my friends. I don't have a wife or a girlfriend so I guess that's something to work on. When it comes to family I love my father, but not as much as I should. Maybe this trip is my opportunity to work on my relationship with him. As I think about him I decide that I should probably give him a call and let him know that I'm close.

An hour and a half later we enter the Flagstaff city limits and I tell Bill to take exit 195 and head north into the heart of Flagstaff. Not far from Interstate 40 on Milton Road is a Denny's where I'm meeting my father. As we enter the parking lot I see my father standing in front of the place by the front door. Bill stops and I jump out. I grab my pack, thank Bill for the ride, and shut the door.

I walk up to my father who I hardly recognize. He looks forty years older than when I saw him last. He is thin and what little hair he has is white as snow. He is wearing jeans and a flannel shirt. Under that he is wearing a black t-shirt that says "FUCK CANCER" in large white letters on the front of it, which makes me smile. He is also sporting a pair of brown Birkenstock sandals, with socks, which I hate, and of course his signature black rimmed glasses.

"Father."

"Son. How was the ride?"

"Good."

"Good. Hungry?"

"Starving." I say as we head inside.